EMERGENCY: SINGLE DAD, MOTHER NEEDED

BY
LAURA IDING

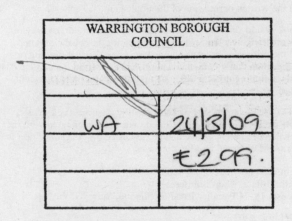

™ MILLS & BOON®
Pure reading pleasure™

All the characters in this book have no existence outside the imagination of the author, and have no relation whatsoever to anyone bearing the same name or names. They are not even distantly inspired by any individual known or unknown to the author, and all the incidents are pure invention.

First published in Great Britain 2009
Harlequin Mills & Boon Limited,
Eton House, 18-24 Paradise Road, Richmond, Surrey TW9 1SR

© Laura Iding 2009

ISBN: 978 0 263 86832 6

Set in Times Roman 10½ on 12¾ pt
03-0309-43433

Printed and bound in Spain
by Litografia Rosés, S.A., Barcelona

EMERGENCY: SINGLE DAD, MOTHER NEEDED

Michele, I love you.
Thanks for being my sister and my best friend.

PROLOGUE

JT STOOD outside in the cemetery between his Uncle Gabe and his grandma. The man wearing all black except for a white collar was talking about what a wonderful person his mom had been and how much she'd be missed. He dug the toe of his shoe into the soft earth, sad because he already missed his mom. He had been waiting and waiting at Uncle Gabe's for her to pick him up. But she hadn't come.

Uncle Gabe said JT was going to live with him now. He was glad 'cos he liked Uncle Gabe but he still thought maybe his mom might come. They told him his mom was up in heaven but he didn't know why they had to put her in the ground first. Maybe she'd be so good in heaven that God would send her back down to earth to be with him.

Grandma was crying. JT felt bad. He'd cried when they'd first told him how his mom had got hurt but now he couldn't cry anymore. There was a heavy rock sitting on his chest, but he couldn't cry.

He tipped his head back, looking up at the tops of the

trees near the gravesite. Was his mom already up there, looking down at them? Uncle Gabe had explained all about how heaven worked. Uncle Gabe said that his mom would always be there for him, watching over him like an angel. JT wished she didn't have to be an angel.

He wanted her to come back and be his mom.

Something small moved near the gravestones. It looked like a baby kitty, except the face had dark circles around the eyes. Not a kitty, but a baby raccoon. He watched the way the baby raccoon moved one way and then the other, as if it might be confused.

When the man in black stopped talking, the grown-ups came over to talk to Uncle Gabe and Grandma. JT ducked away when no one was looking. When he got close to the gravestone he discovered the baby raccoon on the ground was shaking as if it were scared.

Maybe Uncle Gabe would let him keep the baby raccoon as a pet? JT crossed over but the baby raccoon tried to get away, hiding in the grass. He quickly caught it in his hands, but it nipped at his finger. Surprised at the sharp pain, he let it go.

JT sucked the small drop of blood off his finger and watched the baby raccoon run away. Maybe it was too young to be a pet. He thought it must be a boy raccoon, lost and missing his raccoon family.

Just like he missed his mom.

CHAPTER ONE

One month later...

DR. HOLLY DAVIDSON hadn't even hung up her coat on the back of her office door when her pager chirped. First day on the job as the pediatric infectious disease specialist at the Children's Medical Center and she was more than a little nervous. She glanced at the text message: *Stat ID consult needed in ED.*

Okay. She blew out a breath. Guess she didn't have to worry about keeping busy. Trying to ignore her sudden anxiety, Holly tossed her purse into the bottom desk drawer and then quickly headed down the hall toward the elevators.

Several people nodded or smiled at her as she passed them. The anonymity of working with a sea of faceless strangers was a welcome blessing after the speculative looks and abruptly dropped conversations she'd endured for the year after her divorce.

She jabbed the elevator button with more force than was necessary. Well, now things would be different.

She'd come home to Minneapolis, Minnesota after five and a half years to make a fresh start, and to keep an eye on her ailing mother.

Keeping her chin up, Holly entered the busy arena of the ED. A couple of residents hovered around the central nurses' station, laughing and talking with the nurses. She wanted to warn them not to mix business with pleasure, but doubted her wise advice would be welcome.

"Excuse me, I'm Dr. Davidson. Which patient needs an ID consult?" she asked the unit clerk seated like a queen on her throne at the center of the main desk.

"Just a minute," the woman muttered, before picking up the constantly ringing phone. "Emergency Department, this is Susan. May I put you on hold for a moment? Thank you." Susan didn't seem at all frazzled as she glanced up at the list of patients. "ID consult? Mark Kennedy in room twelve."

"Thanks." Holly let Susan go back to her incessant phone calls and walked over to the computer terminal near room twelve, one of the many isolation rooms they had in the ED. She needed to get a little more information about her patient before she examined him.

She logged into the system, relieved her brand-new passwords worked without a hitch, and quickly entered Mark Kennedy's name to access his current medical record information. He was a fourteen-year-old who'd just entered his freshman year at a boarding school. He'd been brought in for nausea, vomiting, severe headache and stiff neck, complaints he'd had for the past two to three days.

Bacterial meningitis? Or the less severe viral meningitis? She hoped the poor kid had the less serious type but was afraid it was more likely he had bacterial meningitis, given his history of being a freshman in boarding school. They needed a lumbar puncture to make a definitive diagnosis. Had one been done? She scrolled down to read the notes, seeing there was a notation about the LP being performed. The name of the ED attending physician, Dr. Gabriel Martin, registered just as a deep male voice behind her said her name.

"Holly?"

Her heart leaped at the familiar sound of Gabe's voice. She had to brace herself before turning to face him, knowing the smile on her lips couldn't possibly be reflected in her eyes. "Hello, Gabe. How are you?"

The shock on his face didn't make her feel any better. "You're back?"

"Yes. I moved home a few weeks ago. My mother has some kidney failure as a result of her diabetes."

"I'm sorry to hear that."

They stared at each other for a long moment, the awkwardness painful. Hard to believe they had once been friends. A friendship she'd helped to ruin, long before Gabe had walked out as the best man on her wedding day.

"It's good to see you." His statement was polite but the reserved apprehension on his face said just the opposite. "Welcome home."

"Thanks." She hadn't been prepared to see Gabe again, assuming he'd moved on with his life and his

career. Since he was still here at the Children's Medical
Center, his career obviously hadn't changed. On a
personal level, though, she suspected they were both
very different from the carefree residents they had once
been. She swallowed hard and looked over toward the
isolation room. "Is Mark Kennedy your patient?"

"Yes." Gabe appeared grateful to get things back on
a professional note. "He's a fourteen-year-old boy who
just moved into a boarding school dormitory six weeks
ago. His symptoms are pointing to bacterial meningitis."

She nodded. "I agree, although we need to isolate
whether the source is Neisseria or Streptococcus. I'm
leaning toward the latter, since it's often the cause of
dormitory-related infections. Do you have the results of
his lumbar puncture yet?"

"No." Gabe glanced at the computer terminal, which
still displayed Mark's information on the screen. "When
I reviewed his history and examined him, I requested he
be placed in isolation. Several of the nurses may have
been exposed, though. If he does have bacterial meningitis, they'll need prophylactic treatment."

"Of course. You'll need treatment, too." She turned
toward the isolation cart, opened a drawer and pulled out
a face mask, gown and gloves. "Have you started him
on antibiotics yet?"

"No. I thought I'd wait for your recommendation
first. Especially as I don't know the type of bacterial infection we're fighting."

"Start him on broad-spectrum antibiotics," Holly
advised, trying not to notice Gabe hadn't changed much.

Tall, with dark brown hair, bright blue eyes and broad shoulders, he had a rugged attractiveness that she'd always been drawn to. Maybe there were a few more wrinkles around his eyes, but otherwise he looked good. Too good. Distracted, she focused on the situation at hand. "Mark has already had symptoms for almost three days. I'm worried he's going to take a turn for the worse if we don't get a jump on this."

Gabe nodded, agreeing with her recommendations. "I'll get the antibiotics ordered right away."

"Great." Once all her protective gear was in place, Holly stepped into the patient's room, leaving Gabe to enter the antibiotic order in the computer.

"Hi, Mark. Mrs. Kennedy." She felt bad for the patient and his family, and could empathize with how it must feel to end up with an infectious disease. "My name is Dr. Holly Davidson. I'm the infectious disease specialist here."

"Yes, Dr. Martin told me he was calling in a specialist." Mark's mom looked upset, her eyes red as if she'd been crying. "Is my son going to be all right?"

"I hope so. We're going to start treating him immediately." She approached the bed, shifting her attention to the patient. Gently, she placed a hand on his arm. "Mark? Can you hear me?"

The boy was very lethargic as he opened his eyes and slowly turned his head toward her. "Yeah," he whispered.

Her stomach clenched. The poor boy was much worse than she'd originally thought. There was no indication in the record that he was this out of it, so maybe his neuro status had only just started to deteriorate. "Mark, we're going to need to start an IV in your arm to give you antibiotics." As she spoke, his eyes slid closed and he didn't respond. She hid a flash of panic. "Mark? Are you all right?"

"Yeah." He answered without opening his eyes.

She felt for his pulse, reassured herself that it was beating steadily beneath her fingers. She turned toward his mother. "Mrs. Kennedy, Mark seems to be getting worse. I'm worried the infection is affecting his brain."

Mrs. Kennedy's eyes widened in alarm. "What does that mean?"

"Just that the sooner we can start the antibiotics, the better." As she finished speaking, a nurse came into the room carrying IV supplies. As she finished her exam, the nurse prepared to place the IV catheter into the antecubital vein in Mark's arm.

"Mrs. Kennedy, I'm worried about you and your family. If this is a bacterial infection, as we suspect, it's highly contagious. You'll need to wear a face mask to help protect yourself from getting sick."

The woman paled. "Contagious? What about the rest of my family?"

"I'm afraid they may need treatment, too." Holly made her tone as reassuring as possible. "The good news is we can treat all of you so you won't get sick. How many siblings does Mark have?"

"Two younger sisters. They're only five and seven, children from my second marriage."

"All right, we'll make sure everyone gets the medication they need. And we'll probably need to tell the school too. His roommates may also need antibiotics."

The nurse placed the IV in Mark's left arm, the boy barely flinching as she slid the needle into his vein. Once the IV was running, Holly hurried out and grabbed more protective gear for Mark's mother, helping her to put the items on.

The mask was the most important piece, and Holly reiterated the need to keep the face mask on at all times.

Gabe walked into the room, carrying the mini-bag of IV antibiotics. The nurse took the bag from his hands and hung it on the IV pole, reprogramming the pump accordingly.

"Please, take a look at him. I think his mental status is much worse," she said in a low tone.

Gabe approached Mark, calling his name just as she had earlier. After a quick exam, concern shadowed his eyes. "He needs to be intubated." He glanced at the nurse. "Melanie, will you grab the intubation bin?" He turned toward Mark's mother. "Mrs. Kennedy, I need to put a breathing tube into Mark's throat to protect his airway. He's so lethargic I'm afraid he's going to stop breathing. I've already made arrangements for him to be transferred to the PICU."

Watching Gabe in action, Holly had to admit he was impressive. Especially the way he took the time to explain everything to Mark's mother. Emergency medicine wasn't her specialty and she stepped back to stay out of the way and to give him the space he needed to take care of Mark, but Gabe stopped her. "Holly, wait. I'll need your help."

"Of course." Her earlier anxiety returned as she walked back toward the bed, watching Gabe set up his equipment with deft fingers. She placed a reassuring hand on Mark's arm, hoping and praying that somewhere deep down he'd feel her touch. "Mark, we're going to place a breathing tube in your throat. It will be uncomfortable for a few minutes, but then your breathing will be much better." Mark didn't indicate that he'd heard her but that didn't mean much. He might not be able to make his muscles obey his commands.

"Help me position his head. With his stiff neck, I'm going to have trouble getting his head tilted to the correct angle."

She understood Gabe's dilemma, and moved over to help. The nurse sat next to Mark's mother, who'd started to cry. Holly wanted to cry right along with her but focused instead on helping Gabe place the lifesaving breathing tube in Mark's throat. Gabe's face was close to hers, the worry in his eyes contagious.

"A little more," Gabe said urgently, as he tried to slide the breathing tube down. "I can't quite get it."

Mark's neck muscles resisted the movement as she struggled to tilt his chin toward the ceiling. She met Gabe's eyes over his face mask. "I can't move his head back any more without hurting him."

Gabe nodded. "All right, then, we need a paralytic. There's some succinylcholine in a vial on the table. Give him a milligram and see if that helps."

Holly's hands were shaking as she tried to draw up the medication. She hadn't been this involved in an emergency situation since she'd been a resident. The medication would help relax Mark's muscles, but it would also stop him from doing any breathing on his own. She injected the medication and shot an apprehensive glance at Gabe. "How long before it works?"

"Not long." He met her gaze, as he gave Mark several deep breaths, using the ambu-bag. "Are you ready?"

She nodded. After the third big breath, Gabe set the mask and ambu-bag aside and she helped tilt Mark's head back to the correct angle. This time she was able to give Gabe the extension he needed. He slid the breathing tube into place, and pulled out the stylet. "Hurry. Hand me the ambu-bag."

After disconnecting the face mask from the end, she handed him the bag. He clipped a small device to the end of the endotracheal tube before connecting the ambu-bag, giving several deep breaths. The end-tital carbon-dioxide detector turned yellow, showing the tube was in the correct place. "Listen for bilateral breath sounds, just to make sure," he told her.

She tucked her stethoscope into her ears and listened as he gave more breaths. She nodded and folded the stethoscope back in her pocket with a sigh of relief. "Sounds good."

"Melanie, call for a portable chest X ray," Gabe directed. "And get a ventilator in here."

"We have the breathing tube in place, Mrs. Kennedy. Mark's breath sounds are good. I know this is scary, but Mark is better off now with this breathing tube in place." Holly did her best to reassure her.

"We'll give him some sedation too, so he doesn't fight against the breathing tube," Gabe added.

"Thank you," Mrs. Kennedy whispered.

Holly was glad to help. She reached over to hold the ET tube while Gabe secured it in place. "Nice job," she said in a low tone. Gabe's quick action had helped to save Mark's life.

His eyebrows rose in surprise and his gaze warmed, lingered on hers. "Thanks."

For a moment the years faded away, the easy camaraderie they'd once shared returning as if it had never left. She'd missed him, she realized with a shock. She'd missed Gabe's friendship.

And more? No. What was she thinking? Taking a quick step back, Holly decided it was time to leave.

"I'll check on the LP results," she murmured, before leaving the room. Glancing back over her shoulder, she saw Gabe was watching her with a speculative glance.

Her stomach tightened as she let the door close behind her and began stripping off her protective gear. She and Gabe had grown close in those months up until her wedding. But that had been nearly six years ago.

She'd learned two hard lessons since then. Men couldn't be trusted and never, ever mix personal relationships with professional ones.

Unfortunately, Gabe lost on both counts.

Gabe instructed the respiratory therapist on the vent settings he wanted Mark to be placed on and spent a few minutes reassuring Mark's mother that they were doing everything possible for her son. He took the time to make sure Mark was comfortable and that his vitals were stable before he left the room. While stripping off his protective gear, he glanced around the ED arena, disappointed to realize Holly was gone.

He opened Mark's electronic medical record and read her note. She recommended changing the antibiotics now that the LP results were back, confirming streptococcal meningitis. She went on to recommend prophylaxis to any exposed staff and for all of Mark's immediate family.

He finished arranging for Mark's transfer to the PICU, and then followed up with the nursing staff who'd been exposed to Mark before he'd been placed in protective isolation. He wrote prescriptions for Mrs. Kennedy's family and one for himself.

Once he was caught up with his work, he went over to the unit clerk. "Will you page Dr. Holly Richards for me again?"

Susan, the unit clerk, frowned at him. "Holly who? You mean the infectious disease doctor? Dr. Davidson?"

Davidson? She'd changed her name from Richards to Davidson? Had she been wearing a wedding ring? He didn't think so. The truth hit him like a brick between the eyes. Holly must have divorced Tom, taking back her maiden name.

Guilt burned the lining of his stomach as he realized her divorce might be a part of the reason she'd returned home. He furrowed his fingers through his hair, not entirely surprised by the news.

Damn. It wasn't too hard to figure out what had happened. He'd bet his life savings Tom had cheated on her. The jerk.

Guilt swelled again, nearly choking him. He should have handled things differently. Why had he believed Tom when he'd claimed he'd changed? Tom had always been too much of a womanizer, and Gabe suspected Tom hadn't changed, even after Tom had asked Holly to marry him. But he hadn't had any proof, just the deep niggling suspicion that wouldn't go away.

On the day of Holly and Tom's wedding, he'd noticed Tom flirting with Gwen, Holly's maid of honor, and confronted him. They'd argued bitterly. Tom had sworn he'd given up other women, promising he'd gotten them out of his system once and for all. Gabe hadn't believed him, telling Tom how Holly deserved better. Tom had turned the tables on him, accusing Gabe of wanting to cause trouble as he desired Holly for himself.

The accusation had been painfully true. More true than he'd wanted to admit.

He'd known the wedding was a mistake, but had figured there wasn't anything he could do about it. But as the hour had grown closer, he'd realized he couldn't stay. Couldn't stand next to Tom at the altar as his best man, watching Holly marry a guy who didn't deserve her love. So he'd handed the rings to one of the other groomsmen and left the church. In some perverse way he'd hoped Holly would get the message and do the same.

But he'd learned later that she hadn't walked away.

The wedding had gone ahead as planned. She and Tom had moved to Phoenix, Arizona shortly after the wedding, so Tom could take a position as medical director of a large surgical intensive care unit while Holly had taken a critical care fellowship position.

Only now she was back, as Holly Davidson rather than Holly Richards. And she was an infectious disease specialist, not a critical care intensivist.

"Did someone page?" Holly asked, walking back into the arena. She'd come from another room, and he felt foolish for interrupting her while she was seeing another patient.

"I did." He hated this feeling of unease between them. "When you're finished, will you give me a call? I'd like to talk to you."

"I'm ready. I just need to write my note." She was looking at him with a puzzled expression, as if she couldn't quite figure out what he wanted to discuss. No surprise, since he wasn't sure what he was going to say to her once they were alone either.

Regret, mingled with guilt, continued to weigh on his shoulders. He couldn't help feeling her divorce was his fault. Especially since he suspected Tom's infidelity might have started before the wedding. Maybe he could have prevented her from marrying Tom if he'd really tried.

"I'll wait." Luckily, the ED wasn't too busy. He'd seen and written orders on all the patients who'd been brought back so far. Mark was the only serious case needing his attention.

Holly strode to the closest computer and signed in.

His gaze roamed over her familiar features. She was more beautiful than ever. Her shoulder-length dark hair framed a heart-shaped face. Her dark brown eyes were always warm and smiling.

"Has Mark taken a turn for the worse?" she asked, logging off the computer.

"No, I just sent him to the PICU." He took Holly's arm and steered her toward the physician lounge, grateful to find it empty. "And I changed his antibiotics, as you suggested."

"Good. I'll go up to visit him in the PICU later. I'm still very worried about him, I hope he turns around with the antibiotics soon." She glanced around at the empty lounge, then back up at him. "So what's up?"

He hesitated. There was so much he should say, but part of the problem was that he should have told her his suspicions a long time ago, even without proof to back up his claim. Yet just like all those years ago, the words seemed to stick in his throat.

She sighed and jammed her hands into the pockets of her lab coat. "You don't have to do this," she said slowly. "I already know why you left the church the day of my wedding."

His mouth dropped open in surprise. Had Tom told her about their fight? If so, he'd no doubt left out key details. "You do?"

She nodded, finally bringing her gaze to his. "It was my fault. Because of the night I ruined everything by almost kissing you."

CHAPTER TWO

THERE. She'd said it. Boldly brought up the night she'd crossed the line, ruining their friendship, forever.

After admitting the truth, Holly felt as if a huge weight had rolled off her shoulders. It was good to have everything out in the open between them. At first she'd been so angry at Gabe for walking out on her wedding, until she'd realized it had been her own fault.

Looking back, she realized she should have taken her subtle feelings toward Gabe, and his subsequent leaving of the church, as a sign. Especially after the horribly public and painful way her marriage had ended. Still, wasn't it always easier to look back after the fact, to realize what you should have done?

"Holly, it wasn't your fault at all."

He was just saying that to be nice. The night she'd almost kissed him, he had been the one who'd pulled back, who'd stopped her from making a terrible mistake. She hadn't even had a good reason, the situation hadn't started out as anything more than two friends going to check out a band for her wedding. Tom had been called into surgery, so Gabe had gone with her instead. They'd crashed the wedding, had a few drinks and danced, deciding then and there to hire the band. She'd only intended to thank him for coming along. But the moment she'd looked up into his dark eyes the atmosphere had changed. Suddenly she'd wanted to kiss him. Had actually leaned toward him, until he'd pulled back, making her realize what she'd almost done.

Afterwards, she'd been horrified at her near miss. And, right or wrong, she hadn't said anything to Tom. What could she say? That she'd almost kissed his best friend? She hadn't, but being tempted even for a second was bad enough. She'd tried to brush the whole episode off as a foolish mistake, a result of too much wine, but that moment in time had bothered her long afterwards.

"When did you divorce Tom?" he asked.

Her eyes widened. Good grief, had the news of her divorce traveled all the way across the country? A note of panic laced her tone. "What makes you think I divorced him?"

For a moment he looked taken aback by her question. "Because you're using Davidson, your maiden name."

She let out an exasperated huff, realizing she'd overreacted. Thank heavens the gossip mill hadn't reached this far. She didn't want Gabe to know the gory details. "Not all women take their husband's name," she pointed out. After the divorce she'd wished she hadn't, as changing her medical license in both the state of Minnesota and the state of Arizona had been a pain. "But you're right. Tom and I split up almost two years ago."

"I'm sorry," he murmured.

He was? She ignored the tiny pang of disappointment. "So am I. But I'm over it now." She didn't care about Tom anymore. Any feelings she'd had for him had been wiped out by his betrayal.

But she didn't think she'd ever get over losing her daughter. The familiar wave of grief tightened her stomach. She'd wanted children so badly, had been so thrilled to become pregnant. Looking down into her daughter's sweet, tiny face and knowing she'd been too young to survive had been heart-wrenching.

She'd never forget Kayla. Lost in the sorrowful memories, she belatedly realized Gabe was staring at her. With an effort she tucked her daughter back into a protected corner of her heart and glanced around. "I, uh, need to get back to work."

"Wait." He held out his arm, stopping her from brushing past him. "I'm sorry, Holly. You have every right to be angry with me."

"I'm not," she protested. His fingers were warm against her arm and she must be pathetic and desperate to wish he'd haul her close. She needed to get a grip on her emotions and keep a polite distance between them. "Honest." She stuck out her hand. "Friends?"

He stared at her outstretched hand for so long she feared he wasn't going to take it, but then his large hand engulfed hers, easing her inner tension. "Of course, Holly. I'll always be your friend."

"Good." One could never have too many friends, right? She missed her friend Lisa from Phoenix, but somehow suspected Gabe wasn't going to be able to fill that role. She shook his hand firmly, before stepping back. Nothing good would come of rehashing the past. Moving forward was what was important. Taking this position at the Children's Medical Center was a huge step forward in her career. Now that she was here, she wanted to do a good job.

And if that meant working with Gabe on a professional level, then fine. No problem.

"Gabe?" One of the nurses poked her head into the lounge. "There's a call for you. It's JT," she added when he looked as if he would brush her off.

He nodded and turned away. "I have to take this, Holly. Excuse me." Without waiting for a response, he strode out to the closest phone.

Curiosity compelled her to follow him, shamelessly listening to his end of the phone call. "JT? What's wrong?" He paused. "Another nightmare? Hey, it's all right, buddy. I understand. I'm glad you called, see? I'm here at work. Everything is fine. I love you, JT."

Holly sucked in a harsh breath, shock rippling all the way down her body to the soles of her feet. From the tone of his voice and the brief reassuring conversation it was easy to deduce JT was a young child.

His son. Gabe must have a son.

Which meant he was likely married, too.

A stab of disappointment pierced her heart, stealing her breath.

"Maybe you'd better let me talk to Marybeth, okay?"

Gabe said in a cajoling tone. "Don't worry, I promise I'll run home to see you during my lunch-break."

Holly turned away, feeling slightly sick. Why she was bothered by the fact that Gabe had a son and a wife, she had no idea. He certainly deserved to be happy. But she couldn't help feeling as if the rug had been pulled out from beneath her.

Maybe because Gabe had a family.

And she didn't.

For a moment she remembered the excitement of being pregnant, the thrill of carrying a tiny life in her womb.

But she'd lost her small daughter. And in almost the same moment had lost her husband.

No, a family wasn't in her future.

She must have been standing in a daze because suddenly Gabe was back. "I didn't mean to ditch you like that, but when JT has nightmares, he needs to talk to me right away."

"Sure, I understand. Congrats." She pushed the word through her constricted throat, trying not to dwell on the painful past. "On your marriage and your son."

"I'm not married," he said, a slight edge to his tone. "Marybeth is JT's babysitter."

He wasn't married? Skeptical, she found herself wondering if he was really telling the truth, but then remembered how he'd referred to Marybeth by name. He hadn't said maybe JT should let him talk to *Mom*, he'd said maybe JT should let him talk to *Marybeth*. The difference eased the tension in her chest.

"Sounds like you have your hands full," she murmured. She wondered where JT's mother was. Had Gabe gotten a divorce too? Did they share custody?

"Yeah, a bit." He shrugged, although his expression was still troubled. "I'd ask you out for dinner, but I can't leave JT home alone and his babysitter takes night classes."

Dinner? As much as she was tempted, she knew seeing Gabe outside work was just asking for trouble. The last thing she needed was to be seen with one of her colleagues outside work. Still, it sounded as if he might need some help. And she was more curious than she had a right to be about JT's mother. "It's okay, but if you need help with JT, let me know."

He flashed a lopsided smile. "Thanks. But I think I have everything under control."

Of course he did. Gabe was always strong, and extremely competent. The way he'd taken control with Mark proved that. "See you later, then."

"Take care, Holly."

She turned away, heading back to her office where she'd left the list of patients she was scheduled to see.

The list was long, but that was all right. Better to keep busy than to wallow in the mistakes of the past.

Or to wish for something she could never have.

After he found someone to cover over his lunch-break, Gabe rushed home, knowing he didn't have a lot of time. "Hey, JT, how are you?"

"Uncle Gabe!" The five-year-old threw himself into Gabe's arms. "I missed you," he mumbled against his shoulder.

Gabe closed his eyes, holding the little boy close. The poor kid had been through so much, yet he couldn't keep leaving work every day either. "I missed you too, sport." He hugged JT tight, then eased back to look into the boy's eyes. "You had the bad dream again?"

JT nodded. "Wild animals came out of the woods and tried to bite me."

Gabe didn't understand this sudden fear of wild animals that JT seemed to have. But he suspected the real underlying factor was losing his mother. And worrying if he was going to lose Gabe too. "Last night, before you went to bed, I explained how I had to work today. Remember?"

JT's lower lip trembled, his blue eyes wide. "I know, but when I had the nightmare, I forgot."

"It's okay." He couldn't be mad at the poor kid, after everything he'd been through. When his sister, Claire, had been killed in a car crash, he'd taken custody of JT. His mother, who'd recently moved to Florida and remarried, had offered to move back to help out in raising her grandson, but he'd declined her generous offer. After all these years, his mother deserved to be happy.

So he'd taken JT because there wasn't anyone else. And he'd even gone as far as to apply for formal adoption. He'd managed to get things moving the week after Claire's death but now they were waiting on DNA tests from the two men who, according to his sister's diary, may be JT's biological father. Despite the security he'd tried to give his nephew, JT had a deep fear of losing Gabe in the same abrupt way JT had lost his mom.

He'd hoped the boy's nightmares would fade over time, but so far no luck. Of course, it had only been four weeks since the funeral.

"Everything all right?" he asked Marybeth, JT's babysitter. The girl was a young college student who watched JT during the day and took a graduate class two evenings a week, on Mondays and Wednesdays. He was lucky to have her, especially when she'd established a great rapport with his nephew.

"Fine," she reassured him. "JT is always better once he talks to you."

Crisis averted, at least for the moment. "Do you think he's okay to attend his pre-school this afternoon?"

"Sure. I think he'll have fun."

"Okay, then. I'll pick him up on my way home."

"Let me know if you run into trouble, I don't start class until six o'clock."

"I will." The few times he'd had to work late Marybeth had been more than willing to pick JT up after pre-school. He turned back toward JT. "I'm going back to work now, but I'll pick you up at four. You know how to tell the time, don't you?"

JT nodded with enthusiasm. "Yep. When the big hand is on the twelve and the little hand is on the four." He hopped from one foot to the other, his earlier fears seemingly forgotten. "Me and Jeremy are going to play swords this afternoon."

"Be careful." Why did boys always want to play with weapons? Gabe figured he must have done the same thing at JT's age, but it was amazing how almost anything he gave the boy to play with ended up as a sword, a knife or a gun, no matter how hard he tried to discourage it. Maybe JT could use the sword to kill the wild animals in his dreams. He pressed a kiss on the top of JT's head. "All right, then. I'll see you later, buddy."

"Bye, Uncle Gabe." JT's face was relaxed and smiling, making him feel better about going back to work. As he strode to his car, he noticed he'd barely have time to wolf down a quick sandwich before seeing patients. But the potential indigestion from eating too fast was worth taking the time to calm JT's fears.

Too bad he hadn't been able to ask Holly out for dinner, but leaving JT wasn't an option. The boy's emotional status was still too fragile. Would probably be too fragile for a long time to come.

Yet after meeting Holly again that morning, he couldn't get her out of his mind. Interesting how she'd assumed he'd left because of the moment he'd sensed she'd been about to kiss him when in reality it had been his own response he'd run from. She couldn't know how close he'd come to crossing the line that night, too. Stepping back from her had been one of the hardest things he'd ever had to do.

Tom had been right during their argument on his wedding day. He *had* wanted Holly for himself. But that was then, and things had changed. He wasn't just a single guy anymore, he had JT to think about now. The boy needed a home, stability. Besides, he wasn't still hung up on Holly.

He'd moved on with his life, had been engaged to

marry Jennifer before Claire had died. Their engagement had been broken off when he'd discovered that she hadn't been at all willing to take JT in as their adopted son. She'd kept arguing that they needed to find JT's real father, something he was trying to do. His plan all along, even once they found JT's biological father, was to fight for sole custody of JT.

Forced to make a choice between Jennifer and JT, his young nephew had won hands down. And if the reality of living with a young boy day in and day out was overwhelming, he'd have to learn to deal with it.

He caught a glimpse of Holly leaving the ED and his pulse kicked up in awareness. He took a deep breath, trying to ignore his body's reaction, telling himself it was only physical because he hadn't been with a woman since Jennifer had walked out on him.

There were more important things to worry about than the last time he'd gone out with a woman. Right now, JT had to come first.

With everything that had happened in the past, he knew better than anyone that he and Holly could never be more than friends.

Holly spent the rest of the afternoon trying to keep her mind off Gabe and figuring out how to balance the stat calls with the scheduled patients she needed to see. At three-thirty, her mother called to let her know she was finished with dialysis. Holly had just finished seeing her last patient, so she readily agreed to drive her mother home.

The outpatient dialysis unit wasn't far from Children's Medical Center, so it didn't take her long to get there. She tucked her mother into the passenger seat, and then headed to her mother's house.

Hemodialysis treatments usually left her mother feeling exhausted, but that didn't stop her from asking questions. "How was your first day at work?"

"Pretty good. Busy," Holly answered as she negotiated rush-hour traffic. She cast her mother a quick glance. "I really like my job. I have many interesting cases."

"I'm glad." Her mother smiled faintly, her face pale. "I hope I didn't take you away from anything important."

She thought of Mark, the young boy whose condition was still so tenuous. "No, you didn't. Although I do have a very sick young man in the PICU."

"I'm sure you'll help make him better." Despite her mother's reassuring tone, deep lines of fatigue bracketed her mouth. For a moment Holly felt a flash of resentment toward her father. Her father had been Dr. Kendall Davidson, the chief of neurosurgery and he'd died several years ago after a long night of surgery. Her parents had divorced when she'd still been in high school, a traumatic event when she'd discovered her father had been cheating on her mother. When his young lover had become pregnant, he'd filed for divorce.

She'd made peace with her past, except for rare moments like this, when resentment still burned. How ironic that by marrying Tom she'd made the same mistake her mother had.

Tom had seemed to want the same things she did, a

loving home and family. Children in particular were
important to her, she hadn't wanted to put her kids
through a painful divorce like she'd experienced.

After Kayla was stillborn, Holly had known there
wasn't anything left of her marriage to save. Wisely,
Tom hadn't bothered to put up a fight. To his credit, he'd
made the divorce proceedings as painless as possible.

Pushing the memory aside, she pulled into her
mother's driveway and brought the car to a halt. After
getting sick, her mother had finally given up her mau-
soleum of a house to move into the much smaller, more
practical home located closer to the hospital. So close
she could easily take a care-van to her dialysis appointments. Holly hurried around to open the car door. "Here,
let me help you."

Her mother leaned heavily on her arm as Holly
guided her inside. After she'd got her mother settled on
the sofa, covered in a warm, wool blanket, she went into
the kitchen and threw together a light meal of scrambled eggs and toast, carrying everything out on a tray.

"Thanks, Holly." Her mother's grateful tone made
her feel guilty for leaving during those years she'd been
married to Tom. It was good that she'd come back home.
Obviously her mother needed her.

"You're welcome." She leaned over to give her
mother a gentle hug. "Is there anything else you need
before I go?"

"No, thanks, dear."

"All right, then. Call my cell if you need me." Holly
let herself out of the house, wondering if the time would

come that her mother might need more full-time care. If so, she'd do her best to take care of her.

Family was important, even if her father and Tom hadn't thought so.

Her pager went off and she paused in the driveway to glance at the display. The message wasn't from work, as she'd expected, but rather from Gabe.

Please, call me when you have a minute, Gabe. He'd left his number on the text message too.

Was he still at work? Had something happened to Mark? With a frown, she flipped open her cellphone and dialed his number.

"Hello?"

"Gabe? It's Holly. What's wrong?"

"I picked up JT from his pre-school and something just doesn't seem right. He's running a low-grade fever and has chills." Gabe sounded uncertain, not at all like his usual self. "I don't think it's serious, but I could use a second, unbiased opinion." He paused and then added, "If you're not too busy."

She hesitated for the barest fraction of a second before she realized she was allowing her personal need to stay away from him to interfere with taking care of a sick child.

How could she turn him down? After all, she'd offered her help. "Of course I'm not too busy. I'll be right there."

CHAPTER THREE

HOLLY wasn't sure what to expect when she arrived at Gabe's house. Luckily, his directions had been easy to follow, but when he opened the door before she had a chance to knock, it was clear his usual calm composure had deserted him. He wore a haggard expression and his brown hair stood on end, as if he'd raked his fingers through it non-stop for the past few hours.

"Thanks for coming over." Gabe stepped back to allow her to come in. "I'm pretty sure JT just has a virus, but I want to make sure I'm not missing something, like strep. I've peered down his throat so many times I'm starting to doubt myself."

"That's because you're thinking like a parent, not like a doctor." She'd seen plenty of stressed parents and those with medical backgrounds weren't any different.

"Yeah, maybe." He sighed and scrubbed a hand over his jaw. "I know I'm probably overreacting, but this is the first time JT's been sick."

"The first time, ever?" She was taken aback by the news, considering the boy was five years old. Most kids at least had the occasional ear infection or bout of flu before the age of five. "I'm surprised."

She barely had time to notice the warm, welcoming earth tones of his living room before he dragged her down the hall to his son's room. "I'd like you to take a look at him. My first instinct was to treat him with a pain med and wait to see how he does overnight, but he's been so listless I've started to doubt my objectivity. Be honest. Tell me if you think I should take him into the clinic."

"All right." Odd, it wasn't at all like Gabe to doubt himself. He was after all board certified in emergency medicine. Taking care of sick kids was his specialty.

But, then again, she'd made similar mistakes with horrible consequences. Assuming her cramping pains during her pregnancy had been from stress and not from placenta previa, a condition where the placenta broke away from the wall of the uterus prematurely. She'd downplayed her situation and had lost her daughter as a result.

Even if she had gone to seek help earlier, there really hadn't been a chance of saving the baby, not at only twenty-five weeks gestation. Still, her medical knowledge hadn't helped her then.

Gabe's might not be helping him now either.

He pushed open the door to a small, cozy bedroom. "JT? Hey, buddy, this is Dr. Holly. I've asked her to take a look at you."

"Hi, JT." She approached the boy, who was curled up on the bed.

"Hi." His dark blue eyes, so much like Gabe's, stared up at her. "I don't feel so good."

"So I hear." She sat on the edge of his bed, noticing his face was flushed. She offered a reassuring smile. "Does anything hurt you?"

"My head hurts."

"Hmm. How about your throat?" She felt his forehead, noting he was indeed running a slight fever but not one that was dangerously high. She trailed her fingers down to his throat. No swollen glands from what she could tell. "Can you open wide for me?"

Obediently he opened his mouth. "Ah-h-h."

Using her penlight, she peered down his throat. No sign of any infection at all, from what she could see. Although maybe it was too early to tell. "Great job. How about your tummy? Does that hurt?" She gently palpated JT's abdomen, and he didn't wince, neither did she find any enlargement of his liver.

"No, just my head. The lights are too bright."

Hmm. Strange that he would have photosensitivity. She spent another minute or so examining him, but didn't find anything seriously wrong. His pupils were equal and reactive. Yet, like Gabe, she sensed something just wasn't quite right. She glanced back at Gabe, who hovered over her shoulder. "You treated his fever?"

"Yeah, I gave him a dose of pediatric pain med right before you came over."

"Good." JT closed his eyes, either because the light was too bright or he was simply tired and falling asleep.

"He was fine at noon when I came home for lunch," Gabe muttered. "Suddenly I pick him up from his pre-school class and he's running a fever and not acting at all like his usual self."

"I'm sure it's just a virus," she assured him.

"So you don't think I need to take him in?" Gabe asked.

She hesitated for a moment, and then shook her head. "No, I think I'd wait and watch him. If his headache persists tomorrow, though, I'd take him in. Kids do get headaches with fevers." She rested her palm against JT's flushed cheek for a moment, thinking how young and innocent he looked.

JT's eyelids fluttered open. "You're pretty," he murmured.

His sweet expression tugged at her heart. It was no secret where the boy had gotten his charm. "Thank you."

She glanced up to find Gabe watching her intently.

"JT obviously has good taste," he murmured in a low tone.

Raising a brow, she didn't try to come up with a response. Since JT was starting to doze off, she gently stood and tiptoed out of the room. Gabe followed her, softly closing JT's door behind him.

By mutual consent, they moved into the living room so they wouldn't wake him. Gabe's expression held chagrin. "I suppose you think I'm an idiot for calling you over."

"Not at all." Holly subtly looked for pictures of JT's mother, but didn't find any. "I'm sure it's not easy being a single parent."

"No, it's not." Gabe dropped onto the sofa with a sigh. "I don't know what got into me, but suddenly I was staring down at him, thinking the worst. And then I thought of how stupid I'd look if I took him in for nothing. But if you hadn't answered your page, I probably would have risked it."

"Hey, it's all right. I really don't mind." She sat in the matching love seat across from him. "I know it's none of my business, but where is JT's mother?"

Gabe stared at his hands for a long minute, before lifting his head, his eyes dark with pain. "She died in a car crash less than five weeks ago."

"How awful," she murmured, thinking it was a good thing JT had someone like Gabe as his father.

"Yeah, it's been a little rough, more so for JT." Gabe abruptly stood. "Are you hungry? I made some spaghetti for dinner but JT wasn't hungry. The least I can do is feed you for your trouble."

His abrupt change of subject caught her off guard, but hearing that JT's mother had died so recently she supposed she couldn't blame him for not wanting to talk about it.

Gabe headed for the kitchen, leaving her little choice but to follow him. She knew being here with him was like tempting fate to repeat itself, but the spicy garlic and oregano scents drew her forward.

"Have a seat." Gabe waved at the small, oak kitchen table. "This will only take a few minutes to warm up."

Her stomach chose that moment to rumble loud enough for Gabe to hear. Leaving now that he knew she was famished would be too obvious, so she sat. "Guess I am a bit hungry after all," she admitted with a sheepish smile.

Gabe flashed a grin and opened his fridge. "Let's see, I really wish I had a bottle of fine Italian wine to offer you, but it seems all I have at the moment are two of JT's favorites, grape juice or milk. Take your pick."

She laughed. "Gosh, tough decision. I'll choose milk."

"Milk it is." He pulled out the container and filled up a large glass, setting it in front of her. "The pasta should be done in a few minutes. At least I have home-made garlic bread."

The butter and garlic scent was already filling the kitchen, mingling with the zesty spaghetti sauce. "Smells delicious. I had no idea you could cook."

"Pure necessity for two bachelors living on their own." Gabe stirred the sauce and then pulled out two plates. He dished out the pasta and sauce, adding a large chunk of fresh garlic bread to each serving.

Her mouth was watering as he set down her plate and then sat across from her. He lifted his milk glass and touched the rim to hers in a quick toast. "Thanks, Holly. I appreciate you coming to my rescue."

She rolled her eyes in exasperation before taking a sip of her milk, suddenly glad they weren't drinking anything stronger. The last time she'd shared a few drinks with Gabe she'd foolishly attempted to kiss him. "You and JT would have been fine. The worst thing that might have happened is that you'd have taken JT to the clinic for nothing more than a virus."

"Maybe," he conceded, his gaze holding hers. "But it was still nice to have someone else to talk to."

The poignant sadness lurking in his eyes made her wonder if Gabe was still in love with JT's mother. He'd claimed he wasn't married, but did that mean they were divorced? Or was he a widower of only a month? If so, all the more reason to keep her distance from him emotionally. Gabe was in no position to start a relationship, even if she was willing to risk one.

Which she wasn't.

"Eat," he urged.

The sooner she ate, the sooner she could leave. She dug in, nearly closing her eyes in ecstasy when the taste of the tangy tomato sauce exploded in her mouth. "Mmm. This is divine."

"Glad you like it." Gabe grinned, and instantly the flash of sorrow was gone. "It's an old family recipe from my mother's side. She's a great Italian cook."

She widened her eyes in surprise. "I didn't know your mother was Italian."

"Absolutely." Gabe gestured with his fork. "Her maiden name is Fanelli. She's living with her new husband down in Florida."

"And your dad?" she asked, before she could think.

His expression closed. "He's been out of the picture for a long time."

"I'm sorry." She reached for his hand, realizing she'd touched a nerve. Yet it was a bit surprising to realize she and Gabe had something in common. Apparently neither of them had been close to their fathers.

He held her hand in his for a long minute. Her heart thudded in her chest as the light-hearted mood turned into something more serious.

"Uncle Gabe?" JT's plaintive cry broke the moment. "My tummy hurts."

"Uh-oh, maybe he's going to throw up." Gabe jumped up from his seat at the table. "I'll be right back."

Confused, she sat back in her seat, staring after Gabe as he disappeared down the hall to JT's room.

Uncle Gabe? She'd assumed JT must be his son, but obviously the boy was really his nephew. Still, he was caring for JT, so he must have custody. She knew she should admire the close bond they shared, but couldn't help feeling resentful.

Somehow it didn't seem fair, that Gabe had the joy of love and caring for JT while she'd lost her daughter.

Gabe sat beside JT but the boy didn't vomit. The bed was damp, though, so he helped JT change his pajamas and then stripped the sheets off the bed, replacing them with a spare set from the hallway closet.

"Hey, buddy, maybe you should try to eat. Your tummy might hurt because you're hungry." Gabe tried not to wince at the mountain of laundry growing larger by the minute. It seemed as if he had constantly been doing laundry since JT had moved in. Not that he was complaining, but in the battle between him and the washing-machine, he rarely emerged the winner. "I can make you some chicken noodle soup, your favorite."

"No, I don't think so." JT scrunched down into the covers, blinking owlishly against the light. "Is the pretty lady still here?"

"Dr. Holly?" Unable to squelch a flash of guilt, settled on the edge of JT's bed. Since taking custod his nephew, Gabe had never invited a woman over.

now. Logically, he knew JT was too young to understand the potential implications, but he intended to set a good example for the boy, anyway. "Yes, she's still here. Why, did you want to ask her something? Does your throat hurt now?"

"No." JT shook his head. "But I like her. She seems nice."

"She is nice." Oh, boy. They were treading on dangerous ground here. Gabe tried to think of a way to prevent JT from getting the wrong idea. "She's a good doctor. She often takes care of sick kids, just like you."

"Oh." He could see the wheels turning in JT's mind. In a disappointed tone the boy asked, "She's a real doctor?"

"Yep. She's a real doctor, just like me. We work together at the hospital."

JT bit his lower lip, his gaze wistful. "Do you think she'd come back and visit once I'm better?"

She would, he knew, if only for JT's sake, but the knowledge made Gabe hesitate. He'd give anything to help JT deal with his nightmares. At the same time he wasn't willing to start something he couldn't finish. "I don't know, she's pretty busy. Why don't you get some sleep, hmm?"

JT nodded, pulling his green and yellow stuffed dinosaur close, the one Claire had given him. The toy had been his constant companion over the past few weeks. Gabe brushed a kiss over JT's forehead before getting to leave.

"G'night, Uncle Gabe," he whispered.

"Goodnight, JT."

Outside JT's room, he leaned back against the door and stared at the ceiling. JT was seeking a mother substitute because he missed his mother. As JT's grandmother lived in Florida he didn't get to see her that often. Obviously, JT approved of Holly.

He couldn't blame the kid. He did, too.

Blowing out a heavy breath, Gabe dropped his head and rubbed the back of his neck. There was no way to explain to JT that bringing a woman into the mix was the wrong idea. He knew from experience that not all women were willing to raise someone else's son.

Heck, he was struggling a little with the reality of being a parent and he already loved his nephew.

It would be better for both of them if he and JT stuck it out alone. Maybe he should move to Florida? JT's grandmother could fill the motherly role.

Using Holly wasn't an option.

Strengthening his resolve, he hustled back to the kitchen, where he'd left Holly. When he walked in, the first thing he noticed was that she'd cleaned up his entire kitchen. Very nice, considering he wasn't exactly a neat cook.

"You didn't have to clean up," he protested.

She lifted a shoulder, avoiding his gaze. "It's all right."

He hesitated, realizing Holly was upset. Was she upset that he'd put JT first, rushing off to take care of his needs? No, he couldn't believe Holly was that much like Jennifer. She looked more upset than angry.

"What's wrong?" he asked, as she carefully folded his dish towel and hung it on the drying rack.

Holly turned to face him, her eyes full of reproach. "Why didn't you tell me JT was your nephew?"

Damn, he'd forgotten. He hadn't wanted to push JT to call him Dad, not when he'd known him all along as Uncle Gabe. "JT is Claire's son."

His sister's name caused her expression to soften. "Oh no, Claire? Claire is the one who'd died in a car crash?"

Holly had only met Claire once, so it wasn't too surprising that she hadn't jumped to the right conclusion right away. If he was honest, he'd admit he hadn't tried very hard to clarify the truth either. "Yes. I took custody of JT the same day."

"I'm sorry." Remorse filled her face. But then she frowned, her expression more hurt than puzzled. "But, Gabe, why didn't you tell me? You must have known that I'd assume JT was biologically your son."

The hurt in her eyes made him want to cross over to her, but after the conversation he'd had with JT he forced himself to stay where he was. One brief visit and JT was already wondering if the "pretty lady" would come back again. He never should have called her over here. Getting close to Holly wasn't an option. "Maybe I should have told you. I've petitioned the court to formally adopt him."

"What about JT's biological father? Doesn't he want custody?" she asked.

"No." His answer was evasive and he knew it. JT's biological father was the last subject Gabe wanted to talk about—it was one complication he refused to discuss, especially with Holly. Not until he had the DNA results back. He didn't want to hurt her unnecessarily. "Right now, I'm the only family JT has, besides his grandmother. I can't just let him go to some stranger."

"I understand." Holly's gaze warmed, her earlier pique forgotten. "I admire you, Gabe. It takes a special man to step up in a crisis. I think you'll be a great father."

"I hope so." He wished he could be so sure, especially considering he hadn't had a good role model. Balancing the effort of raising JT and work wasn't easy. In fact, days like today he wondered if he was cut out for the job.

Holly's willingness to come over helped, though. And her kind words touched a place in his heart he thought he'd closed off a long time ago. He missed the closeness they'd once shared. The night they'd danced together, during the wedding they'd crashed to see a band, was permanently etched on his memory.

"Hey," she said, bringing him back to the matter at hand as she smiled gently. "You'll be fine."

He nodded, glad she hadn't reacted negatively, the way Jennifer had. Except for that brief moment when she must have assumed he'd lied to her on purpose. But Holly's appreciation was almost harder to take. Desperate for distance, he edged toward the front door. "Thanks again for coming out, and for cleaning up my messy kitchen."

"You cooked. Besides, I needed something to do." Holly caught his hint, picking up her purse and following him through the living room. At the front door though, she paused and glanced up at him, her c scent wreaking havoc with his brain. "Gabe?"

He braced his arm against the doorjamb, trying not to let her sensual scent overwhelm his common sense. "Yeah?"

"I'm sorry. I was upset, partially because I thought you lied to me about JT on purpose."

His fingers curled into a fist to keep from tucking her hair behind her ear, tipping her face up to his. "I didn't mean to."

"I know. It's just that I've been lied to a lot in the past." Her earnest gaze held his. "Thinking you had lied to me too…" She let her voice trail off.

For a long moment he stared down at her. Tom's infidelity had done more damage than he'd realized, to her self-confidence and her self-esteem. "Holly, you deserve better. Don't sell yourself short. Ever."

Her sad smile ripped at his heart. "I'll try."

She moved as if to open the door. He didn't make a conscious decision to stop her, but he must have because suddenly she was in his arms, her soft curves pressed against his hardness, her mouth sweet yet passionate beneath his.

CHAPTER FOUR

LOST in wonderful, myriad sensations, Holly reveled in the kiss. Until a tiny corner of logic deep in the recesses of her mind forced her to realize what she was doing.

As much as she wanted to kiss him, heavens, she loved kissing him, Gabe was wrong for her. Starting something on a personal level with him would only end badly. For her. Bringing her hand up to the center of his chest, she gave a weak push. He reacted instantly, breaking off the kiss and taking a quick step back, stumbling, nearly falling in his haste to get away.

She felt lost without his arms supporting her. Missed his warmth, his heady desire. Trying to gather her reeling senses, she whispered, "We can't do this."

"No." Gabe surprised her by agreeing, as he blew out a heavy breath and scrubbed a hand over his jaw. "We can't. I'm sorry."

Sorry he'd kissed her? Or sorry it had been the wrong time and place for both of them? She should be glad she was the one who had been strong enough to end insanity but instead she only felt cold. Bereft.

Every neuron in her body tingled from the effects of his kiss. That a simple kiss could affect her so deeply, knocking her off balance in a way Tom's kisses never had, frightened her.

"I have to go." Blindly, she turned and headed for the door.

"Holly." Gabe's voice stopped her. Steeling herself against a strong desire to throw herself back into his arms, she glanced over her shoulder at him. "If things were different, I'd ask you to stay."

Her knees wobbled as a fresh wave of desire curled in her belly. She wanted to deny how much she wanted him, but she couldn't lie. Not about this. "If things were different, I might."

For the longest moment they stared at each other. But Holly knew standing there and wishing for things to be other than what they were was absolutely useless. So she turned and continued outside, heading to her car.

She could feel Gabe's gaze on her back, but she didn't turn to look. Heaven knew, she didn't want to see the same longing she was feeling reflected in his eyes.

Coming out to help him with JT had been a mistake.

Somehow, some way she needed to forget those brief moments of pure heaven she'd spent in Gabe's arms.

Holly was relieved she didn't get called down to the ED again the next day. Avoiding Gabe would help re-establish equilibrium. Maybe if she was lucky, she wouldn't to see Gabe the rest of the week.

On Thursday afternoon she went up to check on Mark. His mother was alone, seated at his bedside in the PICU.

"Good afternoon, Mrs. Kennedy." She flashed a warm smile. "How are you holding up?"

Her response was a wan smile. "I'm fine. It's Mark I'm worried about."

Placing a hand on the boy's arm, Holly gazed down at him, feeling helpless. The antibiotics should be fighting the infection by now. His neuro status should be starting to improve.

But it wasn't.

"Mark?" She tucked her hand around his. "Can you hear me? Squeeze my hand."

Nothing. She bit her lip and tried again. "Mark, wiggle your toes. Come on, show me how you can wiggle your toes."

Still no response. She pressed her thumb into the back of his hand and he pulled away from the slightly painful stimulus. At least that much of a response, withdrawal from pain, was a little encouraging.

"He's not getting any better," Mrs. Kennedy said in a low voice. "And it's all my fault."

What? Holly left Mark's side and crossed over to his mother, crouching in front of her to take the woman's hand. "Mrs. Kennedy, don't blame yourself. It's no* your fault Mark contracted a bacterial infection."

But the woman was shaking her head. "I'm the c who agreed to send him to boarding school. It was husband's idea. He thought the structure of a mi* boarding school would be good for Mark, but in

I think maybe he just wanted my son out of his hair." Her voice broke and she tugged her hand from Holly's grasp and buried her face in her hands, sobbing quietly.

Knowing very well how easy it was to wallow in guilt, Holly put her arm around the woman's shoulders and hugged her. "It's not your fault. There are plenty of kids who go to boarding schools every year, and they all don't get meningitis." She didn't add the fact that bacterial meningitis was more common in dormitories and there was a vaccination against it. The poor woman felt bad enough. "And do you know how tough it is to raise teenagers these days? I have to say, your husband might have had the right idea, putting him in a structured school right from the beginning. A good friend of mine had so much trouble with her teenage son she often wished she'd done something like that right from freshman year."

Mrs. Kennedy sniffled and raised her tear-streaked eyes. "Really?"

"Yes, really." Plucking a box of tissues off the counter, Holly handed them to her. "Please, don't feel guilty. Mark needs you to be strong. There's still a chance he can pull through this. Hang in there with him, okay?"

She blew her nose and nodded. "I will."

"Does your husband come to visit Mark?" Holly asked, trying to get a feel for the family dynamics. She hadn't been lying about her friend's troubles with her but there may have been a grain of truth to what Mrs. Kennedy had described. It could be that her husband had wanted her son from her first marriage out of the way.

"He wanted to, but I wouldn't let him." Mrs. Kennedy sniffled again. "Maybe structure is good for teenage boys but I still think he just wanted to get rid of Mark."

Mark's illness could easily drive a wedge in the family. "Mrs. Kennedy, your marriage isn't any of my business and I'm not trying to pry, but it's at times like this when you need to come together as a family. Do you love your husband?"

Wordlessly, she nodded.

"Well, then, don't hold this against him. Blaming him or yourself isn't going to help Mark at this point." Holly didn't want to see this family fall apart. If Mark did pull through, he'd need both his parents' help and support. She was a firm believer that kids deserved an intact family, she'd often wished she'd had one. "My advice is that you let your husband visit Mark. He should be here with you, or at least relieve you so you can spend time with your other children. You need to lean on each other, get all the support you can."

Mrs. Kennedy's eyes filled with cautious hope. "Do you really think so?"

"Yes. I do." She reached over and gave the woman another hug before rising to her feet. "I'm going to ta￰ to Mark's critical care physician, see if there's anyth￰ else we can do. Take care of yourself, all right?"

She nodded. "Thank you."

"You're welcome." Holly left the room, w￰ her eyes, which were starting to brim with t￰ felt so bad for Mrs. Kennedy and for Mark. ￰ ficult situation.

After conversing with the critical care physician in charge of Mark's care, they agreed to reduce his sedation to see if they could get him to be more responsive. Holly had also insisted on another CT scan of his head. She wondered if he was suffering from an increase in brain tissue swelling.

Trying not to dwell on the seriousness of Mark's situation, Holly continued the rest of her rounds. She was just finishing a consult note on a young girl with a fever of unknown origin when her pager went off.

She read the text, her heart sinking. The call was from the ED. Full of trepidation, she finished her note requesting an MRI brain scan and then called the ED. No reason to worry, there was a good chance Gabe wasn't working today. "This is Dr. Davidson from Infectious Diseases. Did someone page?"

"Holly?" Gabe's familiar voice echoed in her ear. "I need your help. We have a serious situation down here."

"What is it?" She straightened in her seat, alarmed by his grave tone.

"I have three Hmong children all showing signs of active tuberculosis."

"Active TB? Are you sure?" Her heart sank in her chest. Active tuberculosis was rare, except in certain nt populations. This was serious, especially if the g children had been exposed by an infected adult.

sure." Gabe's tone was grim. "They all have d a cough, two of the older ones tested positive PD skin test, but the youngest is only four and ative. We've had chest X rays done and are treating them aggressively, even the youngest one. But there are about twenty family members packed in the waiting room and it's likely one of the adults is the primary source of the infection."

Dear God. Hmong families tended to stick together, everyone showing up at the hospital when one loved one was ill. And they often lived together too, many people crammed into small residences. Fertile ground for fostering infection. The possibility of a sick adult spreading tuberculosis to more children here at the hospital was horrifying. Having three infected children was bad enough. "Do whatever you can to isolate the family. I'll be right there."

Gabe had never been in such a volatile situation before. The implications of extensive TB exposure was overwhelming. Even now he could see there were at least fifteen to twenty other people in the ED waiting room, and if any of them had been close to the source of infection, they would need treatment.

After donning a face mask, he ushered the family into a large conference room where he could at least shut the door. It didn't have negative pressure, as dictated by hospital code, but it was better than nothing.

"My name is Dr. Martin and I'm afraid the thr girls you brought in, MeeKa, BaoKa, and YiKa, all h tuberculosis. Tuberculosis is a very serious and contagious lung infection." He scanned the room. center of the group, his gaze rested on the oldes ber of the family, the grandfather, whose p sunken eyes, and deep rattling cough triggered his internal alarms. "Sir?" He approached the elder. "How long have you had that cough?"

A woman stepped up. "Excuse me, Tou Yang doesn't speak any English. I can tell you my father has been feeling bad for a long time, many weeks. Tou Yang has refused to go to the hospital to see a doctor, though."

The Hmong were a very patriarchal society, so he understood how it might be that no one in the family dared to go against the grandfather's wishes. With a sinking heart he realized they'd have to force the man into treatment in order to preserve the health of the community.

Where was Holly? He glanced at his watch. Despite the kiss that had shattered his piece of mind, he was anxious for her help. He really could use her expertise.

"Gabe?" As if he'd conjured her by will alone, Holly stepped into the room, wearing a tight-fitting face mask just like his. "I've been in touch with health department officials—they're on their way."

Thank heavens.

Holly swept her gaze over the group. "Do they understand they will all need to be evaluated for treatment?" she asked in a low tone.

He shook his head. "Not yet. Although I believe the grandfather is the original source."

Holly stepped forward. "I think Dr. Martin explained the three girls you brought in all have tuberculo-
believe your grandfather has passed the lung in-
to the children. I'm afraid this means you have

all been exposed as well. Each of you will need to be evaluated for treatment."

Those who understood English gasped and several translated to the family members who didn't. Gabe watched the shocked reaction go through the group and knew with a sinking certainty they didn't understand the bigger issue. Treatment for active TB wasn't as easy as taking a pill for a week. The drugs were highly toxic, with many possible side effects, and the usual treatment regimen lasted a full nine months.

The family asked lots of questions. Between them, he and Holly answered them the best they could. Once they had generally calmed the family's fears, Gabe and Holly left.

Outside the conference room, he tugged his face mask off and scrubbed a hand across his jaw. "Now what?" he asked.

Holly stripped her mask off too, taking a deep breath. The masks were very restrictive. "We keep them here until the public health officials arrive. At least most of the family members appeared to be in pretty good health."

Gabe nodded. "I think I'd better give the ED at Minneapolis Medical Center a heads-up. The kids can be evaluated here, but the rest of the family will need be taken to the Center."

"Good idea. And what about the people who we the waiting room when they came in? How on ear we going to identify them?"

He'd had the same concern. "They all have to register when they come in, so we can pull the list of all the people who registered within fifteen minutes of the Yang family, and maybe fifteen minutes afterwards, to capture them all. If the family had pretty much kept the grandfather surrounded, we probably don't have to do much more than TB skin tests on the rest of the people who were in the waiting room."

"All right, let's get that list."

He led the way back to the arena, already feeling much calmer about the situation. How was it that Holly's presence helped him to relax? She'd had the same effect on him last night, dealing with JT's sore throat.

"Dr. Martin? You have a call on line two. Something about being late to get home?"

Damn, how could he have forgotten JT? Appalled with himself, he grabbed the phone and punched the button to connect. "Marybeth, I'm so sorry."

"It's all right, I don't have major plans for this evening." He was so lucky to have someone as understanding as Marybeth helping to watch JT. And it was Thursday, a day she didn't have class. "But JT was worried, so I figured I'd give you a call."

"I understand. Put him on the phone." After a few seconds, he heard JT's voice come on the line. "Hey, Daddy, I'm sorry I got stuck here at work. We have lots of sick kids here who need my help."

"When are you coming home?" JT asked in a plaintive tone.

Good question. One he wasn't sure he had an answer

for. He shouldn't have forgotten about picking him up in the first place. And now, as much as he wanted to be there for JT, he couldn't just walk away from this mess. "I'll be home by six o'clock, okay? Marybeth is going to make you dinner but I promise I'll be home right afterwards."

"Okay. Tell the sick kids to get better."

Gabe had to laugh at the child's logic. If only it were that easy. "I will. See you soon, JT."

He hung up the phone and turned, bumping right into Holly.

"Gabe, I can stay and handle things here." Her compassionate gaze confirmed she'd overheard his conversation with JT. "You should go home."

For a heartbeat he imagined what his life would be like if he had someone like Holly to help him with JT. A wife to come home to, a true partner rather than a college-student babysitter.

As quickly as the tempting thought formed, he pushed it away. JT was fragile enough—the boy didn't need any more complications in his life.

Losing his head and kissing Holly had proved she was a major complication and more.

"I'm staying. But thanks." He forced himself to s⸱ away, more tempted to share his burdens with her ⸱ he wanted to admit. "Let's get this resolved, shall⸱

Holly admired Gabe's dedication, especiall⸱ torn expression in his eyes when speaki⸱ showed how much he really wanted to be h⸱

he didn't take up her offer to cover for him, she left him to take care of the girls while she met with the public health department officials to deal with the rest of the Yang family.

Luckily, the health department agreed with her assessment and, as Gabe had anticipated, got the entire group of adults moved over to a secure location at Minneapolis Regional Medical Center, located adjacent to Children's. Despite his wishes, the grandfather would need to be admitted immediately.

When she had that problem solved, she decided she should check on the three girls, who were the most sick. As she entered the isolation room she found Gabe was already there, holding the youngest girl, YiKa, who was only four years old, against his chest. The tender expression in his eyes squeezed her heart, stopping her in her tracks.

The poignant picture was enough to steal her breath. He was so caring, so compassionate. She could easily see him cradling his daughter the same way.

He was a wonderful father.

JT was very lucky to have him.

She wanted to leave, to wipe this compelling vision ᴉ her mind. Gabe was clearly the father she'd wanted ᴏ be. But instead of being there for her, when the ᴺg pains of her placenta breaking away from her ᴀd started, Tom had been with some other ᴇ'd betrayed her in more ways than one.

ᴿ her shoulders, she fought the sudden urge

to cry. The last thing she wanted was Gabe to see how much his presence affected her.

There was no point in longing for something she could never have.

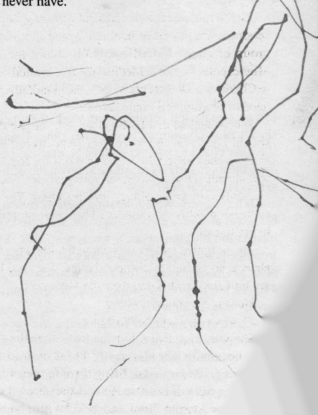

CHAPTER FIVE

HOLLY kept herself occupied with work, the tuberculosis situation consuming most of her time. Thankfully she didn't have to interact with Gabe much, especially once the three girls were admitted up on the fifth-floor general medical unit.

So far the girls were tolerating their treatment well, but it was also very early. Most of the side effects of the medication hit after about a week or so. She'd heard from the public health department that there were two other adults, aside from Tou Yang, who also had active TB, but the rest of the family only needed outpatient prophylactic treatment.

A part of her wanted to tell Gabe the news, yet her part of her wondered if she was simply looking excuse to see him again. There was really no to go down to the ED. She didn't really even work schedule. In the end she decided that if ned to run into him, she'd let him know the the Yang family. For all she knew, he might e news from some other source.

On Friday evening she gratefully wrapped up her first week of work. Mark Kennedy was finally starting to wake up, the infection having been beaten by the antibiotics. Looking back, she wanted to laugh at her initial nervousness. Five days and she already felt like an integral part of the team.

Her first week had been full of challenging cases, what with the meningitis and active tuberculosis.

In less than a week she'd also broken her cardinal rule by kissing Gabe.

She sighed and reached for her purse, knowing she needed to get over this strange obsession with him. He was a friend, nothing more.

Her cellphone rang. She recognized the number and realized the caller was her friend, Lisa Waltrip, from Phoenix, Arizona.

"Hey, Lisa, how are you?"

"Great. Hey, guess where I am?"

Holly frowned. "Um, Phoenix?"

"No, silly." Lisa laughed. "I'm here in Minneapolis. How would you like to get together for dinner?"

"I'd love to!" Holly was thrilled her friend had come to visit. "Where are you staying?"

"At some hotel across from the airport." There was a slight pause. "Ok, I can see a restaurant from my window—a Mexican place called Chili's. Are you in the mood for a margarita?"

Holly laughed. Spending time with her friend was just what she needed. "Absolutely. Would it be all right if I met you there, say, in about an hour?"

"It's a date."

Holly hurried out of the hospital before her pager could go off and keep her from meeting Lisa. On the ride home she called her mother to check on how she was doing. Friday was another dialysis day and because she'd been so tied up with the TB cases, she hadn't been able to give her mother a ride home.

Her mother sounded tired as usual after her treatments, but her spirits were good.

"I'm meeting a friend from Phoenix for—Do you want me to stop by afterwards on my way home?" Holly asked, feeling a little guilty for going out at all.

"Oh, no. Georgia is stopping by. Don't worry about me. Just go out and have fun."

Georgia was her mother's youngest sister. Holly was glad her mother wouldn't be all alone tonight. "All right, but call if you need me."

She ended the call as she pulled into her driveway. Dashing into the house, she quickly changed into a comfy pair of jeans and a royal blue sweater that made the most of her creamy skin and dark hair. For a moment she wished Gabe could see her like that, but then just as quickly pushed the thought aside. What on earth was she thinking? Spending time with Lisa was supposed to help her forget about Gabe, not bring him to the forefront of her mind.

Annoyed with herself, she headed back out to meet Lisa. The traffic was backed up, so she arrived a few minutes late. Standing at the hostess desk, she scanned the restaurant and found Lisa sitting at a table in the middle of the room. She hurried over.

"Lisa! It's so good to see you."

Lisa stood to return her hug and it was then that Holly noticed her friend was pregnant.

Very pregnant.

"Surprise!" Lisa's laughter bubbled out as she stared at Holly's dumbfounded expression.

"Oh. My. Goodness." Holly felt the blood draining from her face and fought to keep her shock from showing in her eyes. She forced a smile. "Congrats." Belatedly she gave Lisa another tight, enthusiastic hug. "When are you due?"

"In two months, just before New Year." Lisa beamed as they took their respective seats. Her pregnancy obviously agreed with her. "I'm ready any time, though."

Holly was happy for Lisa, truly. But at the same time she couldn't deny a twinge of envy. Beneath the cover of the table her hand went to her own stomach, as if seeking the familiar bulge, the reassuring sensation of the baby moving. She'd been thrilled to be pregnant, just like Lisa was, but hadn't made it to her seventh month.

Kayla. Sweet, innocent Kayla. She still had a picture of her daughter, the tiny pink dress they'd put on her and the footprint in clay they'd made, all courtesy of the caring, compassionate nurses in the neonatal ICU.

"Holly?" It took a moment to realize Lisa was talking to her.

"I'm sorry, I was daydreaming for a minute there. What did you say?"

Lisa's smile faded. "You're upset, aren't you?"

"No." Her denial was a little too quick. "Of course not,

Lisa. I'm very happy for you. Honest. Tell me everything. What did Ben say when you told him the news?"

"Holly, it's okay. I understand." Lisa reached across the table to give her hand a squeeze. "I know you're happy for me, but that doesn't mean you don't miss your daughter."

Her throat tightened and she nodded. "Yes, I'll always miss Kayla. But now is not the time for you to think about pregnancy horror stories." Like hers. "Seriously, tell me everything. I know I haven't seen you in about five months, but I didn't even realize you guys were trying to have a baby."

Lisa stared at her for a long moment, and then went into a detailed explanation of the events—how they hadn't really been trying, but had gone on a weekend getaway and had forgotten protection. "I think Ben planned it all along, but I guess I won't complain," Lisa finished with a broad smile. "Having a baby is a perfect way to start the new year."

Holly tried not to think about how she'd lost her baby right before Valentine's Day. Holidays didn't always hold good memories. At least Valentine's Day was nothing special, especially when you were single.

The waitress came and took their order. Lisa requested a non-alcoholic margarita, and Holly did the same.

Her mood was volatile enough, without adding alcohol to the mix. Lisa described how she was really in town for a work-related presentation, but soon the conversation turned back to her baby.

Holly didn't try to stop her from discussing her pregnancy. After all, she remembered what it was like to have a baby be the center of your world. Soon, though, the topic of conversation turned to the people they'd both worked with.

"Kris has been nothing but a pain in the butt ever since…" Lisa's voice trailed off.

"Ever since what?" Holly asked. Kris had been one of the nurses in the ICU who had been extremely annoying to most of the physicians at one time or another. The woman was young but had the personality of a scorpion and always thought she was right, even when she wasn't.

"Never mind." Lisa picked up her drink and took a huge gulp, avoiding her friend's gaze. "It's not important."

Suddenly she knew. "Kris is dating Tom, isn't she?"

Lisa sighed and hung her head. "Holly, I'm sorry. I wasn't going to bring it up."

"It's all right." Holly picked up her water, wishing it was full of whiskey. "My marriage to Tom is over."

"True. And, really, Kris is such a witch, she deserves him. She should know better than to marry a guy like Tom, especially knowing his reputation."

Holly carefully set her water glass down. Little had she known Tom's reputation had been common knowledge long before she'd discovered his infidelity. And because she'd been blind to the truth, her reputation had suffered too. It was one of the things she regretted most.

She was fiercely glad she wasn't still in Phoenix, especially now that she knew there was a chance Tom might get married again. If she thought the whispers and stares had been bad then, they'd be a million times worse now. She couldn't bear the thought of people talking about her behind her back.

Holly managed to get through the rest of the meal, but the jeering voices in the back of her mind followed her all the way home.

Poor Holly. Losing her baby and her husband in the same day. How tragic. Too bad she didn't figure out Tom was cheating on her before she got pregnant.

Now she has nothing.

By Saturday Gabe was relieved to see that JT seemed better. His headache was gone but the boy was still more tired than normal. JT had a Cub Scout field trip planned at a local dairy farm and the boy had been very excited, waiting very impatiently for this day to come.

Gabe struggled with a feeling of strange desolation as he waved at JT, watching him ride off in a large vehicle with a group of five other boys, all from the same pre-school class. Was he a bad parent because he hadn't volunteered to chaperone? Being a guardian to JT was more complicated than he'd imagined. Once again he wondered if he should move to Florida with JT. Staying here in Minneapolis, where JT's life could have almost the same routine as before Claire's death, had seemed to be the best option. So why was he doubting his decision now?

There was plenty to do around the house but, rather than be happy to have the time to himself to get things done, he couldn't escape the feeling he should be spending more time with JT. Originally, he'd been scheduled to work this Saturday but then a colleague had needed to switch weekends so he'd ended up being off. Maybe he should have added his name to the chaperone list for this trip, even if it had been at the last minute.

Deciding he was doing his best at being a guardian for JT, he picked up the gallon of blue paint JT had picked out for his room and headed down the hall to the bedroom. He quickly pulled all the furniture away from the walls and into the center of the room, then went to work. Slathering paint on the walls was a mindless job, which was good in a way yet he couldn't stop his mind from drifting to Holly, wondering how she was spending her weekend.

She wasn't working the weekend, because he'd checked.

If he was interested in seeing Holly on a personal level, this would be a perfect opportunity, considering JT would be gone for most of the day. What would she say if he asked her out for lunch?

The selfish part of him, the part that relived her kiss over and over each night in his dreams, wanted to see her again, even though he knew that starting something with Holly was the last thing JT needed. JT would latch on to Holly, or any other woman he chose to date, because of how much he missed his mother. Yet at the same time, if things didn't work out, his nephew would be the one to suffer. Logically Gabe understood the dynamics, the reasons he'd made the firm decision to avoid relationships, but that didn't stop him from thinking about the possibilities of seeing Holly anyway.

Once the Yang girls had been admitted to the general floor he hadn't seen Holly at all. He'd missed working with her.

He enjoyed being with Holly, no matter what they were doing. He'd felt that way years earlier, before she'd married Tom, and somehow the passing of time hadn't changed a thing. If anything, the desire to be with her only seemed to have grown stronger. Especially since their kiss.

Because she was free, no longer engaged to his friend.

But now he was the one with responsibilities. An emotional young boy, suffering from nightmares and reeling from the recent loss of his mother. A boy who desperately needed a parent to hold on to.

Painting JT's room didn't take long, and as he cleaned off the bright blue paint rollers, he inwardly debated whether he should call Holly or not. Was he being selfish if he stole a little time for himself?

He called Holly's cellphone and was disappointed when she didn't pick up, the call going directly to her voice mail. He left a brief message before hanging up, trying to be relieved to know the decision had been taken out of his hands.

Then he remembered how Holly had mentioned her sick mother, suffering from diabetes and renal failure. Knowing Holly, she was likely over there now, taking care of things.

Her mother didn't live far away—he remembered

being there prior to Holly's wedding—so he drove past, just to see if his suspicions were correct.

They were. Holly was outside, wearing a bright red jacket, her dark hair falling freely to her shoulders, her cheeks pink from the wind as she raked leaves around the base of a large maple tree. He pulled up in front of the house, thinking she was fighting a losing battle because the wind kept blowing the leaves away from her pile. He climbed out of his car, intending to help.

"Hi, Gabe." She seemed surprised to see him, but leaned on her rake as if glad for the break. "How are you? Is everything all right with JT?"

"Yes, he's fine." He gently tugged the rake from her hands and picked up the chore where she'd left off, sweeping all the leaves into a large pile. "JT's on a Cub Scout trip to the dairy farm."

"Great. That must mean he's feeling better."

"He is." Gabe tried to block the wind with his body, but dozens of leaves danced along the yard regardless. He grimaced, reaching out with the rake again. "I don't think we're going to get them all."

"No, probably not." Holly glanced around, propping her hands on her slim hips. She was so beautiful, with her eyes sparkling in the crisp fall air, she took his breath away. "Guess this means we have no choice."

"No choice?" He didn't understand.

"No choice but to jump." She let out a laugh and in a carefree movement that reminded him of JT plopped into the large pile of leaves. Still giggling, she picked up a pile of leaves and threw them at him.

The smell of the earth, intermingled with the crunching of the dried leaves, took him back to his own childhood. When he and his sister, Claire, had spent hours playing in the leaves in their front yard beneath twin oak trees.

"Hey," he protested lightly, grinning at her antics. Unwilling to be left out of the fun, he tossed the rake aside and jumped in beside her.

When she let out a startled cry and rolled into him, he put his arms out to help protect her. Laughing when their limbs became tangled, her efforts to get free only brought them closer. When she ended up in his arms, practically on top of him, he realized his mistake. Or his good fortune.

Her laughter faded as she gazed down at him, unaware or uncaring how leaf fragments clung to her hair. His chest tightened and he knew this was exactly what he'd wanted. Why he'd come to find her.

"Holly," he murmured, reaching up to thread his fingers through her hair and slowly easing her head down until her lips met his.

This time their kiss was even more explosive, his senses reeling as Holly's breasts pressed against his chest. Gabe growled low in his throat and deepened the kiss, exploring her sweet depths the way he'd wanted to before. Unlike the last time, Holly didn't resist.

Closer. He wanted more, wanted to feel every inch of her body against him, so he rolled, switching places so he was on top, the leaves providing a soft cushion from the damp ground. He kissed her again and again, barely pausing to breathe, desperately wishing he could make the barrier of their clothes disappear.

"Gabe." Holly moaned his name when he trailed a string of kisses to the soft spot beneath her ear. When he scraped his teeth against her skin, she gasped and writhed beneath him.

He wanted to take her home. Now. To his bedroom.

A car drove by and the driver beeped the horn twice, breaking the moment. He glanced up in time to see the teenage boy behind the wheel flashing a leering grin and a thumbs-up sign.

He wanted to laugh, but Holly stiffened beneath him and suddenly gave a Herculean push against his chest. He moved aside and she scrambled to her feet.

"What's wrong?" he asked, moving much more slowly, thanks to his almost painful arousal.

"I— We— Anyone could have seen us." Holly was brushing leaves off her clothes, tugging the hem of her jacket down. "I have to go."

"Go?" Call him slow, but he didn't understand what in the world had her so upset. "Go where? I thought…?"

"You thought wrong. This shouldn't have happened." Her about-face, changing from the woman who'd shivered and moaned in his arms to the woman glaring at him as if he'd committed some horrible crime, confused the hell out of him. She turned and headed toward the house.

"Holly, wait a minute." He tried to stop her, but she ignored him, disappearing inside her mother's house and closing the door behind her with a decisive and final click.

CHAPTER SIX

MORTIFIED, Holly leaned against the closed door, covering her burning cheeks with her hands. What had she been thinking to roll around in the leaves, kissing Gabe? Had she completely lost her mind? And what if someone from work had driven by, instead of some teenager? She could already hear the whispers if anyone had seen them together.

She knew comparing the past to the present wasn't fair. The gossip that had surrounded her after Tom had been different. Tom had cheated on her while they'd been married. And she'd been pregnant.

Technically, she and Gabe were free to see whomever they wanted. What they did on their off time should be none of anyone else's business.

Too bad that wasn't the way things worked, especially in hospitals where the employee grapevine was more reliable and saw more traffic than the biweekly administrative newsletter.

The last thing she wanted was for her private life to be in the public spotlight. When she started dating again, she intended to find someone who had nothing to do with her work, preferably not connected with the field of medicine at all. She'd envisioned a lawyer or a banker. Not another doctor. Not Gabe. He was all wrong for her.

"Holly, did you get the leaves raked?" her mother called from the kitchen where she was making a batch of Holly's favorite chocolate-chip cookies.

"Ah, no, it was too windy." Taking several deep breaths, she tried to relax her racing heart, wishing she could dunk her head in a bucket of cold water to douse the flames Gabe had ignited with a mere kiss. Just because she'd temporarily lost her mind, it didn't mean her mother needed to know. She strove for a light tone. "Do you need help with the cookies?"

"Sure, although I'm almost finished."

Shaking off the devastating effects of Gabe's kiss wasn't easy. Hiding her trembling hands in a sink full of sudsy water to wash dishes helped.

But even as she chatted with her mother, she couldn't get Gabe out of her mind.

Especially knowing that if she hadn't pulled away when that kid had honked his horn at them, the chances were high that they wouldn't have stopped except maybe to move somewhere more private.

And there was a tiny, traitorous part of her that wished they had.

At the end of the afternoon Holly took the cookies home with her, as her mother was diabetic and couldn't eat them anyway. On the way back to her house she stopped at the grocery store, not in the mood to cook but needing something she could throw together for dinner.

Since a salad sounded good, she headed to the fresh produce section and bumped her cart into a guy coming the opposite way.

"I'm so sorry!" she exclaimed.

"My pleasure." The guy was about her age, and very attractive with a wide smile and dark, wavy hair. The blatant approval in his eyes as they focused on her face couldn't be missed, yet she wasn't able to summon an ounce of interest.

He may have been a banker, or a stockbroker, or a lawyer, but it didn't matter. Because he wasn't Gabe. The realization knocked her back a step. "Excuse me." She wheeled her cart around him and crossed straight to the spinach.

The gorgeous man took her brush-off with a casual shrug and headed off in the opposite direction. Rattled, she gathered her salad ingredients and went through the checkout line, feeling slightly sick. Maybe she'd eaten too many of her mother's cookies.

At home, the nauseous feeling in her stomach persisted.

Because as much as she didn't want to be involved with Gabe, or with anyone she worked with, it was obviously too late.

She wasn't attracted to anyone else.

Gabe couldn't stop thinking about Holly, wishing things could have ended differently.

He'd just finished putting the chicken in the oven when JT came home. The child seemed exhausted, maybe some lingering effects of the virus he'd had. He wasn't too tired to give Gabe a big hug. Gabe returned the embrace, telling himself this was all that mattered.

He'd figure out how to be a good father somehow. Maybe he and JT could figure it out together.

"Did you have a good time?" he asked.

"Yeah. It was so cool!" JT was tired, yet he'd clearly had fun as he described everything he'd seen at the farm. "We saw cows, horses, chickens, but no pigs." JT looked perplexed. "The farmer said he didn't have any pigs."

"Bummer." Gabe suppressed a grin.

"We watched the farmer milk the cows, but the milk was gross." JT wrinkled his nose. "It was warm. Yuck."

Gabe had to laugh. "We only keep milk in the fridge so it doesn't spoil."

"And then we saw a baby cow, he was so cute."

"Calf," Gabe corrected.

"Yeah, a calf. Then me and Kyle climbed all the way up to the top of the loft. There was lots of straw up there and it made us sneeze."

Gabe only listened to JT with half an ear because he was distracted by thoughts of Holly.

This had been the second time she'd pushed him away. You'd think he'd get the message she wasn't interested.

Except she'd kissed him back. Had urgently pressed against him in a way that couldn't be mistaken for anything but interest.

Until the car driver had beeped his horn.

"Is supper ready?" JT peered at the oven. "I'm hungry."

"Almost." Gabe focused on finishing his dinner preparations, including mashing the potatoes and cooking the broccoli, JT's favorite vegetable because he liked the way they looked like little trees.

JT continued to talk about his trip, more about the antics in the car on the ride up than anything else. After dinner was bathtime.

JT splashed in the tub and Gabe sat on the lowered seat of the commode, thinking about the long, lonely night ahead of him. JT was already yawning, the adventures of his day catching up with him. No doubt he'd be asleep well before his usual eight o'clock bedtime.

He noticed JT kept dropping the soap. At first he thought the boy was just too tired to get a grip on the slippery bar, but then he noticed JT eventually picked it up with his left hand.

But the boy was right-handed.

"Is there something wrong with your hand?" he asked, wrapping a large bath sheet around the boy's damp body.

"No. It just feels tingly."

Tingly? Gabe frowned, wondering why on earth JT's right hand would be tingly. Was this some sort of leftover symptom from the virus he'd had? Maybe he should take the boy in to the pediatrician for a good work-up.

Tucking JT in a few minutes later, he sat on the edge of JT's bed. "I'm glad you had fun today."

"Me, too." JT smiled, his eyelids starting to droop. "Did you talk to the pretty lady yet?"

Holly? "Uh, sort of."

"Is she coming over?" JT blinked, trying to stay awake.

"Soon." Gabe felt bad about lying, but he couldn't invite Holly over. Could he? He pressed a kiss on JT's forehead and the boy's arms came up around his neck in a fierce hug. He returned the gesture, hoping that applying for adoption was the right decision, for both of them. "Good night, buddy."

"G'night, Uncle Gabe."

He returned to the living room and stared at the blank TV. He didn't want to watch some brainless show or outdated movie.

He wanted to see Holly. Damn it, there had to have been something more going on this afternoon. She had been as emotionally involved in their embrace as he'd been.

Fishing his cellphone out of his pocket, he dialed Marybeth's phone number. If she was busy, fine. At least he'd tried.

"Marybeth? It's Gabe. Hey, are you doing anything tonight?"

"Well, it is a Saturday," she said in a wry tone, and his heart plummeted.

"I understand." Of course she was busy. What college student wasn't busy on a Saturday night?

"But you're lucky I broke up with my boyfriend a couple of weeks ago so I'm not doing anything but studying."

He pumped his fist in the air and mouthed a silent, "yes." Continuing aloud, he said, "Really? You seriously don't mind?"

"No, I don't mind. I'll come over and watch JT. I can study there just as easily."

"Thanks." Grateful, he hung up and then sprang into action.

He was going to Holly's house to talk to her. And he wasn't leaving until he had answers.

Holly took the pink box off her dresser and carried it into the living room. Lifting the cover, she stared at the meager yet precious contents.

Kayla's picture was on top, her daughter's face relaxed and at peace. If you didn't look too closely, you could almost believe she was asleep.

Carefully, she lifted out the pink dress, knowing that she really needed to preserve the fabric in a protective sealed container but unwilling to pack it away just yet. Touching the silky fabric helped her to remember Kayla's birth. Lastly, she lifted out the pink clay footprint, with Kayla's name and birth date incised along the top.

Kayla Marie Richards. She traced the letters of her daughter's name with her index finger, feeling sad. Born February fourteenth, died February fourteenth.

Tears pricked her eyelids and she brushed them away with an impatient hand. She needed to stop wallowing in the past. She loved her daughter, missed her very much, but there wasn't anything she could do to bring her back. Kayla would always live in her heart.

And maybe it was time she started thinking about a future.

She could admit now that she'd overreacted that afternoon with Gabe. She'd taken the opportunity to run because she was starting to care too much.

Kissing Kayla's picture, she packed everything back into the pink box and carried it back to her room. Instead of setting it on the top of her dresser, where she'd always kept it close at hand, Holly took it to her closet and chose the highest shelf, one she could barely reach, and pushed the box way back so it was out of view.

Satisfied, she closed the closet door, wishing it was as easy to close away her past.

Her heart leaped when her cellphone rang. Racing to the living room, where she'd left it, she picked it up and opened it without even looking. "Hello?"

"Holly? It's Tom."

Tom? As in her ex-husband? Shocked, she couldn't imagine why he was calling, they'd only exchanged a dozen words, all very polite and civilized, in the two years since their divorce. "Is there something wrong?" she asked, thinking it had to be serious, like his mother was ill or dying, for him to call.

"No, but I'm trying to get in touch with Gabe. Have you seen him?"

All the air left her lungs. Did Tom have some sort of latent psychic ability to know she'd spent a portion of the afternoon rolling in the leaves with Gabe? "Why do you think I know where Gabe is?"

"Holly, it's a simple question." Tom's tone was irritated. "If you don't know where he is, just tell me."

"I don't know where he is." Holly was still having trouble comprehending how Tom and Gabe must have kept in touch all this time. And wasn't it interesting how Gabe hadn't mentioned a word? "Did you try him at home?"

"Yes. Never mind, I'll just leave him a message. Sorry to bother you." He hung up.

Her doorbell rang, and with a frown she glanced at the clock. It wasn't that late, only eight-thirty, but she still glanced through the window, surprised for the second time that day to see Gabe.

She opened the door, not feeling very gracious. "What are you doing here? Where's JT?"

"Hi, Holly. May I come in?"

Sensing he wasn't about to leave without talking to her, she opened the door. "Is this about Tom? Because he just called here, looking for you."

"Tom?" Gabe's frown was genuinely puzzled. "Called for me? Why?"

"I don't know." She closed the door behind him. "Are you telling me you guys haven't kept in touch?"

"No. I've only spoken to him a couple of times out of pure necessity." Gabe took a seat on her sofa. "I walked out on the wedding, remember? We argued. We haven't exactly been on friendly terms."

"I see." Maybe she shouldn't have doubted Gabe. Knowing Tom, he probably wanted some sort of favor. Why she'd been blind to her ex-husband's selfish tendencies she had no idea. Feeling awkward, she stared at Gabe. Why was he there? "Do you want something to drink? I have a bottle of wine chilling in the fridge."

"Really?" Gabe brightened. "That would be great."

Still somewhat confused by Gabe's presence at her house this late, she went into the kitchen for the wine. Gabe took it from her fingers. "Do you have a corkscrew?"

What was it with men needing to be in charge even of something as simple as opening a bottle of wine? Suppressing a sigh, she opened the drawer and handed him a corkscrew, then went to another cupboard for the wineglasses. Gabe deftly opened the wine and she waited while he poured.

"Cheers." He lifted his glass and she had to smile when she remembered how they'd done this same thing at his house with milk.

"Holly." Gabe's expression turned serious. "I'm sorry about this afternoon."

"You are?" Her left eyebrow arched skeptically.

He stared at her for a minute. "No, not really." At her look of astonishment, he went on, "I mean, I'm not sorry I kissed you. Dammit, I've done nothing but dream about kissing you. But something happened—one minute you were in my arms, the next you were running as far from me as you could possibly get. I'm sorry for whatever I did to make you run."

"You didn't do anything." Holly carefully set her wineglass on the counter. How could she explain what she wasn't sure she understood herself? "It's me, Gabe. I don't want to get involved with anyone from work."

He was silent for a moment. "So you're telling me if I worked at some other hospital in the city, things would be different?"

Spoken so bluntly, her reasoning did sound ridiculous. They both specialized in pediatrics, and there was only one children's hospital in the Twin Cities area. But feelings and emotions weren't always logical. She lifted a shoulder. "I guess. Yes, things might be different."

"So it was the driver honking at us that freaked you out."

His persistence was annoying but he deserved the truth. "Look, Gabe, I've had enough of gossip to last me the rest of my life."

"Gossip?" He took another sip of wine, gazing at her over the rim. "Because of Tom?"

She sucked in a harsh breath when he nailed the truth.

His eyes filled with compassion. He set his own glass aside and crossed over to her. "Holly, I'm sorry. What happened?"

She didn't want to tell him, but then realized if she did explain all the gory details, he'd understand why her request wasn't unreasonable. "I was pregnant, about twenty-five weeks along, when the cramping pains started. At first I thought it was just that I needed to rest, but they got worse. I was at work, so I found myself a wheelchair and called Tom's cellphone."

Gabe's hands were suddenly holding hers, tightly.

"He didn't answer, and didn't answer. So I called my doctor and she came running over to push me up to the labor and delivery area. My friend Lisa was with me, too. I kept calling Tom, leaving frantic messages as I knew he wasn't scheduled to do surgery that day. As it happens, there is a whole suite of on-call rooms along the hallway leading to the elevators to go up to L and D. I could hear a cellphone ringing from one of the rooms and suddenly the door opened, and Tom was telling a completely naked, tiny blonde female OB resident how he had to leave."

Gabe's hands tightened on hers, and he swore under his breath.

"Looking back, the expression on his face when he saw me sitting there in the hall outside the call room was pretty comical. But then the pains got bad, really bad, and I was rushed past Tom into the delivery room. My daughter was stillborn. At twenty-five weeks, Kayla Marie was too young to live."

CHAPTER SEVEN

GABE couldn't believe Tom had been so cruel, so callous as to blatantly have had an affair where he worked. Where they'd both worked. And hearing Holly's story made his suspicions about Tom's infidelity prior to his marriage to Holly all the more damning. He knew he should probably tell her his suspicions yet at the same time there was no sense in hurting her any more. Not until he had proof. She'd been through enough pain.

No wonder she'd freaked out when the car driver had honked his horn at them. Tom's affair had been so public, he could easily imagine the extensive gossip she'd endured.

Especially after giving birth to a stillborn baby.

"I'm so sorry you lost your daughter." He couldn't imagine anything worse than losing a child. Especially now that he had JT. "Kayla Marie is a beautiful name."

"She was beautiful." Holly's smile was sad. "But you know what? I grieved more for her than I did for the end of my marriage."

"You had every right to be angry." Gabe found

himself growing more furious by the minute. What in the hell had Tom been thinking? Not only had Tom broken his vows, he hadn't been there for Holly when she'd needed him most.

"Discovering how Tom was having sex with a colleague while I was losing my baby made me vow to never get involved with anyone where I worked ever again."

The anguish underlining her tone tugged at his heart. He understood her logic but didn't like the way she seemed to almost blame herself for what had happened. She deserved better. "Holly, remember how I walked out on your wedding?" When she nodded, he continued, "I had a huge fight with Tom that day, and the fight was about you."

"Me?" Her eyes widened.

"I told him he didn't deserve you. And in turn he accused me of wanting you for myself." He stared into the bottom of his wineglass for a moment, wishing more than anything he'd told her his suspicions before, even without proof. Finally he dragged his gaze up to hers. "He was right. I did want you for myself. I barely held back from kissing you that night we danced, so don't for a moment think I wasn't tempted because I was." His voice dropped to a husky note. "And I always thought you were too good for him."

A tremulous smile played across her mouth. "Thanks."

"You're welcome." He set his own glass aside and approached her, reaching out to tuck a strand of her dark hair behind her ear. Her skin was silky soft. "I guess what I'm trying to say is that I still want you. More than

I did six years ago. But things with JT…" He frowned, reluctant to tell her everything. "Are complicated."

"I see." Although the puzzled expression shadowing her eyes belied her words. "Did you wait until JT was asleep before leaving him with a babysitter?"

"Yeah." He automatically checked his cellphone to make sure Marybeth hadn't called.

"And you came by this afternoon while he was gone on his trip to the farm," Holly said slowly.

He stared at her for a moment. Okay, he could see the pattern for himself, he didn't need Holly to point out the obvious. *Did you talk to the pretty lady? Is she going to come over?* Damn.

"Try to understand. JT's been through a lot these past few weeks. After losing his mom, he's going to be looking for another woman to take her place." He spread his hands wide in a helpless gesture. "I don't want him to get hurt."

The wounded expression in her eyes made him feel like a heel. "And you think I would?"

"No." What could he say to make her understand? Heck, being alone with Holly was making him doubt his own logic. "I was seeing a woman fairly seriously when Claire died. But Jennifer wasn't happy when I brought JT home to live with me. And she didn't want to continue our relationship once she knew I was serious about adopting him."

Holly sucked in a harsh breath. "Why?"

He lifted a shoulder. "She didn't want a ready-made family. But you know what's funny? Like you, I think

I grieved for JT's loss far more than the ending of my relationship. JT was with me. He and I agreed to stick together. Nothing else mattered."

"She was an idiot." Holly's stout declaration made him smile. "She didn't deserve you either."

"JT asked about you tonight as I was tucking him into bed."

A ghost of a smile tugged at her lips. "He's sweet."

"He wants to know if you'll come for dinner." He reached for her hand, knowing he was standing too close to the edge but unable to back away from the cliff. So he took a leap of faith and jumped. "Will you?"

She bit her lip, hesitation in her eyes. "Are you sure?"

"I'm sure." And he was. Sure that he wanted to spend more time with Holly.

"Then I'd love to."

"Tomorrow night?" Tomorrow was Sunday, he'd have plenty of time to run to the grocery store for whatever he needed.

She nodded. "Gabe, I'd never hurt JT."

"I know." He couldn't resist tugging on her hand until she moved closer. Wrapping his free arm around her waist, he pulled her toward him, bending his head to find her mouth with his.

She melted against him and he deepened the kiss, reveling in the heady feeling of having Holly in his arms. He could easily get addicted to holding her, kissing her. For long moments he was lost in the sweet taste of her. As much as he wanted to push for more, to lift her in his arms and find her bedroom, he knew it was too soon.

Breathing heavily, he broke off the kiss, resting his forehead against hers. "Holly, tell me to go home." *Ask me to stay.*

"Go home." But her tone lacked conviction and she curled a fist into his shirt, as if she couldn't bear to completely let go. "What if JT has another nightmare? He'll panic if you're not there."

She was right. As much as he didn't want to leave, he knew she was right. And her concern for JT touched his heart. Holly was nothing like Jennifer. Hope swelled in his chest. This could work.

"Tomorrow night," he reminded her in a hoarse tone, willing his heart rate to return to normal. "Come early."

"All right."

He wanted to kiss her again, but forced himself to let go, to take a step back while he still could. She reluctantly let go of his shirt, smoothing out the wrinkles, and it took every bit of willpower he possessed not to haul her close and kiss her again. "Good night, Holly."

"Good night."

Leaving wasn't easy. Yet even as he drove home, congratulating himself on being smart, Gabe acknowledged he'd taken a big risk in asking her to come for dinner. Imagining JT's reaction was easy. The boy would make more out of the evening than he should.

Taking a deep breath, he let it out slowly. Everything would be fine. He'd just have to explain to JT that he and Holly were just friends.

Yeah. He snorted loudly. Sure. Just friends.

A friend with whom he wanted very badly to make love.

* * *

Holly agonized over whether or not she was doing the right thing, agreeing to have dinner with Gabe and JT.

Gabe's concern for JT was humbling. As much as she resented being lumped in with the woman who'd been stupid enough to leave him when he'd provided his nephew with a loving home, she also understood Gabe's caution was part of what made him a good father.

How could she fault him for that?

Her experience with her own father and with Tom had forced her to believe that most men were extremely selfish. Selfish when it came to sacrificing their family for their own needs.

So far, Gabe's actions proved he was anything but selfish. She admired his dedication to JT.

Gabe had let her know that dinner would be ready at five-thirty in the evening. Earlier than she normally ate but she understood the time would suit JT. Just another example of how Gabe put JT's needs first. At three-thirty, she headed over to Gabe's house, with a container brimming with her mother's home-made chocolate-chip cookies.

"Hi," Gabe's gaze was warm, approving as he opened the door to invite her in.

"Hi." She handed him the container of cookies. "I brought dessert, my mother's home-made chocolate-chip cookies."

"Excellent." Gabe's face lit up. "JT's favorite."

"Is she here?" Holly heard JT ask, seconds before he came dashing across the room. "Hi, Dr. Holly!" He threw his arms around her waist in an exuberant hug.

His enthusiasm dispelled her fears. "Hi, JT." She bent over to return his embrace, poignantly aware of how much she'd lost when Kayla had died. "Hey, you look much better than the last time I saw you."

JT nodded and stepped back. Then he grasped her hand, tugging her farther into the room. "Do you wanna see my new truck?"

"I'd love to." She willingly followed him over to where he'd left a shiny black pick-up truck. Clutching a remote-control device in his small hands, he made the truck spin in a circle and race off down the hall. She laughed. "That's awesome."

"Can I get you something to drink?" Gabe asked.

When she glanced over at him, she noticed a guarded expression in his eyes. Her smile faded. Did he regret inviting her over? "Water would be fine."

"I bought some wine and soft drinks, if you'd prefer."

What she preferred was the grape juice and milk he'd offered her last time. At the very least she preferred a smile. But Gabe wasn't smiling. "Maybe later."

"Look, Dr. Holly, watch this." JT moved the levers on his remote control and the truck spun around again with such force the momentum made it flip over and over several times before smacking into the wall.

"JT, remember I told you to be careful of hitting the walls," Gabe warned.

JT seemed oblivious, more worried about his truck than the wall as he hurried over. Anxiety laced his tone. "Uncle Gabe, I think it's broken!"

"Bring it here." Gabe was calm, reassuring as he sat

on the edge of the sofa while JT ran over with the truck. As their two heads bent over the toy, Holly was aware of how perfect they looked together. No one seeing how Gabe interacted with JT would doubt he was the boy's father in every way that counted.

Ridiculous tears pricked at her eyes and she quickly blinked them away.

The woman who'd walked out on Gabe had to be as selfish as Tom had been. What difference did it make that she wasn't JT's biological mother? He was a precious child, a child any woman could love. Maybe raising children wasn't easy but any woman would be lucky to have Gabe as a partner, as a father for their children.

Wait a minute. The realization made her take a hasty step back, secretly glad Gabe was preoccupied with patiently trying to help JT fix his truck. She didn't want a relationship with Gabe, did she?

The image of the three of them together filled her mind. Her knees felt weak. Yes, she did.

The enormity of what she longed for immediately made her wonder if there was a way to keep their relationship a secret at work. She wouldn't want anyone to know. They would need to figure out how to hide their attraction for each other.

Because she was very much attracted to him. Her intense response to his kisses only reinforced that she had no resistance to him. If Gabe hadn't been the one to stop last night in her kitchen, to break off the kiss and to walk away, she knew exactly what would have happened. They would have made love.

Every cell in her body ached to make love with him.

"There, it's all fixed," Gabe was saying to JT. "Now, remember what I said, don't hit the walls."

"Okay." Relieved, JT came back to Holly. "Da— er—Uncle Gabe fixed it, see?"

Had JT almost called Gabe Daddy? She noticed Gabe freeze in the act of heading toward the kitchen, his expression a mixture of alarm and pleasure when he glanced back toward JT.

"I see." She forced herself to focus her attention on JT. "He's good at fixing things, I bet."

"He had to fix the clothes washer too," JT confided. "But he said a naughty word. Davy at school said that same word and the teacher called his mom." JT's eyes were wide. "Davy got in big trouble."

She suppressed a smile. "I'm sure he did."

Gabe came back with her water. "I can't say anything with Mr. Big Ears around," he muttered under his breath, having overheard JT's story about Davy.

No kidding. She gratefully accepted the water, taking a long sip.

"I hope you like Mexican food," he said, ushering her toward the sofa. "Because JT wanted enchiladas."

"Whatever you make is fine." Holly was pretty sure she wasn't going to be able to eat much anyway. Being here with Gabe and with JT, as if they were a family, was wreaking havoc with her nerves.

What was she doing here?

Could she trust Gabe not to hurt her?

The way he trusted her not to hurt JT?

She thought she'd be able to relax as the evening went on, but instead she became more and more aware of Gabe.

His earlier aloofness faded. Now he was ultraattentive, touching her constantly. A hand against her back as he asked her if she wanted anything more to drink. The briefest squeeze of her hand as he drew her into the kitchen when dinner was ready.

The barely suppressed heat in his eyes as he watched her across the table.

She drank her wine, even though she knew she didn't need the stimulant. Was Gabe sending her a silent message? Did he want her to stay once JT went to bed?

Or was her imagination only playing out her own secret desires?

JT seemed to be a well-adjusted little boy, considering how traumatized he must have been when he'd lost his mother. Obviously, living with Gabe over these past few weeks was exactly what he'd needed.

The three of them played games after dinner. JT's favorite was a board game where one player could bump another player off the board, sending them back to the starting place.

JT enjoyed himself, but he was also a very bloodthirsty player. He bumped both Gabe and Holly off the board as often as possible. When he won, Holly lifted her hands in surrender, deeming him the expert.

When it was time for JT to get ready for bed, he asked if Dr. Holly could tuck him in, too.

Gabe's guarded expression was back as they both

took turns to sit on the edge of JT's bed and give him a hug and a kiss before going to sleep.

They obviously needed to have a talk. But when they returned to the living room, the phone rang. She froze, hoping the caller wasn't Tom. She didn't want the mistakes of her past to taint the possibility of the future. Especially now that she'd had a tiny taste of how wonderful the future could be.

As soon as Gabe answered, though, she knew the caller wasn't Tom. Especially when Gabe asked, "Are you sure you're all right?"

There was another long pause, then he responded, "Don't worry about a thing. I'll figure something out. You just take care of yourself, understand? And let me know if you need anything."

"What's wrong?" she asked when he finally hung up.

His expression was full of concern and he raked his hand through his hair. "That was Marybeth, JT's babysitter. She's in the emergency department over at Minneapolis's Medical Center and needs surgery for an emergency appendectomy."

"Oh, Gabe." Holly understood why he was so upset. "What are you going to do? Are you supposed to work tomorrow?"

"Yes." He sighed. "I'll have to start making phone calls to get someone to cover my shift. And then I'll need to hire a new sitter until Marybeth recovers from her surgery."

If she had been qualified to cover his shift, she would have offered. But she could help Gabe in another way. "I'll stay here tomorrow."

"You?" He frowned. "Thanks, but if one of us is going to call off work, it should be me. He's my responsibility."

"Gabe, I'm scheduled to work next weekend, so I'm off tomorrow."

"You are?" Hope filled his eyes. He came toward her until he was standing so close his male, musky scent clouded her brain, teasing her senses. "Are you sure you wouldn't mind?"

"I don't mind." And she didn't. Watching JT wouldn't be a hardship.

"Holly, I have to be at work early, by seven in the morning." Reaching up, he cradled her shoulders in his hands. "It might be easier for you to spend the night here."

CHAPTER EIGHT

SPEND the night? Had he lost his mind? Had he really just asked her to spend the night?

"I don't know if that's a good idea." The uncertainty in her eyes should have given him the perfect opportunity to back off. So he did. Sort of.

"You can take my bed. I'll sleep on the couch," he said, knowing full well he'd much rather share the bed.

With her.

All night.

Guilt free, as this was really for JT.

"Gabe." Holly's voice was soft, as if afraid she'd wake JT. "You and I both know what will happen if I stay."

He hoped so. He really hoped so. No—wait—that was the wrong answer. Wrong, wrong, wrong. He couldn't spend the night making love to Holly while JT slept blissfully in the next room down the hall.

As much as he wanted to, and he really, really wanted to, it wouldn't be right to let Holly stay.

"Okay, you're right. I don't know what I was thinking." Cool logic finally overrode his libido. He took a deep breath and let it out slowly. She couldn't stay and that was the end of it. "Will you give me a minute to let JT know about Marybeth? I don't want him to be shocked to find you here in the morning."

"Sure."

He walked back down the hall to JT's room. The boy was asleep, but Gabe shook his shoulder and woke him up enough to let him know Marybeth was sick so Dr. Holly would stay with him the next day. JT mumbled something that sounded like "That's good," before he rolled over and went back to sleep.

When he returned to the living room, he was disappointed to find Holly standing near the front door with her coat and her purse, ready to leave.

Because he'd pushed. Too fast.

"Thanks for dinner, Gabe."

Don't go! "You're welcome to come back, any time."

She let out a sigh of exasperation. "You need to make up your mind about what you really want. One minute you're looking at me as if you're not at all happy that JT wants me to tuck him in and the next you're asking me to spend the night."

He swallowed hard, disconcerted that the inner war he'd waged had been so obvious. He knew what he wanted. Holly. In his arms. In his bed.

But unfortunately he suspected that JT wanted something too. A mother. And he couldn't start something with a woman just because JT needed a mother. Holly wouldn't hurt JT on purpose but there were no guarantees. Anything could happen. Especially given the very complicated events surrounding JT's adoption. What if his worst fears were correct? How would he explain to Holly?

If he was right about JT's biological father, he'd lose Holly forever.

He was playing with fire by continuing to see her, but couldn't seem to help himself.

"I know what I want," he admitted. "But you're right, I am worried about how this will affect JT. I think we'd better take things slowly."

Slowly was going to kill him.

She stared at him for a long moment and then nodded. "All right. I'll research some nanny services tomorrow if you'd like." She hooked her purse over her shoulder.

He couldn't let her do that. She was already doing enough by staying here on her day off. JT was his problem, not hers.

"No, I'll do it." The more he thought about his situation, the more he realized he needed to call his mother. He'd avoided taking advantage of her because she'd experienced a difficult life with his father. Now that she'd found and married Hank, she was deliriously happy.

He didn't want to impose on her, but he needed help, at least for a few weeks. This wasn't the best time to bring a new nanny into the picture. JT needed stability. Structure.

Holly left after promising to return at six-thirty the following morning.

Gabe stared out the window, watching her drive away, hoping he wasn't being selfish to take advantage of Holly's generosity.

Finding Holly here the following morning was going to feel to JT as if she'd stayed the night.

Scrubbing his hands over his face, he wished he could erase the image of Holly in his bed. He had to stop torturing himself.

Using Holly as a surrogate mother for JT wasn't smart. He needed to ask his mother to fly up to Minnesota, as soon as possible.

Holly didn't sleep well and it was all Gabe's fault. His ridiculous suggestion to stay the night kept echoing over and over in her head.

When she finally dragged herself out of bed next morning, she had dark circles under her eyes, betraying her restlessness.

After doing her best to hide the effects of her long night, she headed over to Gabe's house. Luckily her normally cheerful nature eroded her crankiness, with a little help from Mother Nature as the sun peeked over the horizon, the sky glowing in glorious pink and orange hues. Sunrises, especially in late fall, were breathtakingly beautiful.

Going over to Gabe's to watch JT was simply helping out a friend. She would do the same for Lisa if she were here. She wasn't getting in over her head.

She parked off to the side in Gabe's driveway, leaving lots of room for him to back out of his garage. She couldn't help shooting a wary glance over her shoulder to make sure no one was watching as she walked up to his front door.

As soon as the thought formed, she became annoyed

with herself. Why did she care what Gabe's neighbors thought? She was here to watch his nephew, nothing more.

Gabe responded quickly to her knock. "Good morning," he said in that sexy, low voice of his. "Thanks again for coming over. I really appreciate it."

"No problem." She hadn't made any firm plans for her day off. Her mother could get a ride to dialysis. Sniffing the air, she homed in on the marvelous aroma of coffee. "Is that coffee?"

Gabe's husky laugh sent tingles down her spine. "Yes. Come on, I'll pour you a cup before I leave."

Sharing coffee in Gabe's kitchen was strangely intimate. She tried to get things back on track. "Anything in particular I need to know about JT?" she asked, sipping the flavorful brew and hoping the caffeine would hit her bloodstream fast.

"Not really." Gabe looked comfortable wearing his dark green scrubs as he leaned against the kitchen counter. "I called my mother last night. She's going to catch the first flight from Fort Meyers, Florida to Minneapolis today so you won't need to worry about wasting any more of your days off."

Spending time with JT wasn't a waste but she thought she understood what he was really saying. He didn't want JT to become too attached to her. Trying to ignore the tiny flash of hurt, she nodded. "Let me know if you need me to pick her up at the airport."

"I will." Gabe set his empty coffee-mug aside and pushed away from the counter. "Don't hesitate to call if you need anything."

Holly followed him to the door and he hesitated for a moment, as if he were going to kiss her goodbye. He didn't, but smiled crookedly as he murmured, "Thanks again, Holly. I owe you one."

Maybe, if she were the type to keep score. But she wasn't. "Have a good day. Don't worry about a thing. We'll be fine."

Gabe hadn't been gone for thirty minutes when JT cried out from his bedroom. Anxious, Holly hurried in.

"JT? What's wrong?"

JT was staring at her blankly, as if he was still half-asleep. She crossed over to sit on the edge of the bed, hesitant to approach too quickly.

"JT, do you remember me? Dr. Holly? I'm here because Marybeth got sick."

His expression cleared. "I remember."

Good, she thought with relief. "Are you all right? Did you have a nightmare?"

JT nodded and moved closer. She wrapped her arm around his shoulders and cuddled him close.

"I have lots of nightmares about wild animals. They bite."

Wild animals? She frowned, wondering what kind of wild animals JT was afraid of. "Yes, I know. But there aren't many wild animals around here."

"I saw a raccoon at the cemetery and my teacher at school says they're wild animals." JT seemed content to stay by her side. "I miss my mom. Sometimes, when I first wake up in the morning, I don't know where I am. And I get worried when I don't see Uncle Gabe," he confided.

She could certainly understand why the boy would have nightmares about wild animals and being abandoned. "I talked to your Uncle Gabe this morning before he went to work at the hospital. If you want to call and talk to him, I'm sure he won't mind."

JT didn't answer right away. "No, I'm okay here with you," he said finally.

Pleased that she'd been able to reassure him, she sat with him for a few more minutes. "Are you hungry? What would you like for breakfast?"

He shrugged against her. "Pancakes?"

"No problem." At least pancakes were easy. She was glad he hadn't asked for something more complicated.

"You smell good, like my mom," he said in a wistful tone.

She caught her breath at his admission, glancing down at his dark blond head tucked against her. The poor kid had been through the wringer these past few weeks.

Maybe Gabe was right to protect his son so fiercely.

And she was wrong. Sitting here with JT cuddled against her, she realized she was already in way over her head.

As the morning wore on, Holly grew more and more concerned about JT. She'd made him pancakes for breakfast, but he ate only a few bites. He also didn't want to play outside, but asked if he could lie on the sofa to watch movies. Halfway through the first one, he fell asleep.

JT's lethargy and poor appetite bothered her. After a brief internal debate, she called Gabe.

"Holly? What's wrong?"

"Sorry to bother you but I think JT's sick again." Holly went on to describe the boy's symptoms. "Remember last time you asked me if he needed to be seen? Well, I think this time he definitely needs to be seen."

Gabe didn't argue. "Actually, I was thinking the same thing. He just didn't seem himself all weekend. I called his pediatrician first thing this morning and have an appointment for tomorrow, but I'll see if I can't get him in today."

Relieved he was with her on this, she added, "I think that's best. Maybe it's nothing but the fact he hasn't been feeling well for a while makes me think there might be something more serious going on."

"I'll call you back." Gabe hung up.

Holly watched JT sleeping on the sofa. He moved restlessly at times, as if he wasn't comfortable. Should she move him to his bed? No, she'd wait to hear from Gabe first.

He called back just a few minutes later. "I have an appointment for him this afternoon at two. I also found someone to cover the rest of my shift. I'm going to pick up my mother from the airport and then head over to get JT."

"We'll be waiting."

Either the airport wasn't busy or Gabe broke speed records getting there and back because he arrived home in just over an hour. Gabe's mother was a plump, petite woman who wore her gray hair short and when she smiled she looked just like Gabe.

"Holly, this is my mother, Isabella Brown. Mom, this is a friend of mine, Holly Davidson."

"Nice to meet you," Holly murmured.

"It's a pleasure to meet you, too." The speculation in Isabella's eyes was hard to ignore. "And where's my grandson?"

"JT?" Holly called. The boy came out of the bedroom, smiling when he saw his grandmother. Still, he didn't run across the room to greet his grandmother with a hug. She cast a worried glance at Gabe. "He's been sleeping a lot and didn't eat much for breakfast or lunch."

Gabe frowned. "Thanks for letting me know."

Watching JT with his grandmother made her realize Gabe had been right to bring his mother up from Florida. Maybe it was best for JT to have his grandmother close by, rather than her.

Sensing she wasn't needed anymore, she took a step back. "I'd better go."

"Thanks again, Holly." Gabe walked her to the door.

"You're welcome." She couldn't help one last glance at JT contentedly seated beside his grandmother. "Will you let me know what the pediatrician says?"

"Absolutely." Gabe gazed down at her. "Actually, depending on what's wrong with JT, I was hoping maybe we could get together later."

He was? A warm glow of pleasure wrapped around her heart. "I'd like that."

"I'll call you." Gabe's low husky voice sent a ripple of tingling awareness down her spine.

Holly couldn't deny she wanted to spend time with

Gabe. Yet it was a little disconcerting to realize Gabe wanted to see her alone, without JT.

She hadn't imagined the banked desire in his eyes. And she couldn't help but anticipate what the evening might bring.

Gabe and his mother took JT to the pediatrician's office. The pediatrician was Dr. Cameron Feeney, a good doctor who Gabe knew fairly well from the Children's Medical Center.

"Gabe, I don't know what to tell you," Cameron said after he'd examined JT. "There are many possibilities. He could have a simple virus. Or a not-so-simple disease such as Guillain-Barré syndrome. I'd like to do a lumbar puncture here to check his spinal fluid, and then refer you to a neurologist."

"He doesn't need to be admitted to the hospital?"

"No, I don't think so. Other than being tired, he seems fine. You could give him a protein drink in his favorite flavor until his appetite improves."

Gabe nodded, hoping JT didn't have anything more than a virus. The possibility of Guillain-Barré syndrome, a disease affecting the nerves of the muscles, causing weakness, had lurked in the back of his own mind, too. The lumbar puncture was rough, but JT was a trouper, getting through the procedure without too much crying.

His mother had cried with JT and afterward declared they needed to stop for ice cream as JT had been so brave. JT polished off his entire ice-cream cone, which made Gabe feel better.

That evening, once JT was asleep and his mother was settled in the guest bedroom, she found him in the kitchen.

"Did you call Holly?"

He raised a brow at her. "Matchmaking, Mom?"

"Maybe." His mother propped her hands on her hips. "What's wrong with a mother wanting to see her son happy?"

He had to admit he'd been thinking about Holly all day. Only concern over JT had taken his mind off her. "JT's sick. I should probably stay home."

"JT's fine. You have an appointment to see the neurologist in a few days. Besides, I heard you tell Holly you'd call her."

Suppressing a sigh, he remembered why he hadn't wanted his mother's help with JT. She meant well, but her dogged persistence drove him crazy.

Still, he had promised. "Okay, fine. I'll call her."

Gabe called Holly's cellphone, pleasantly surprised when she picked up after the first ring. "Hi, Gabe. How's JT?"

"He's fine. The pediatrician did an LP and didn't see any obvious signs of infection. He wants me to take him to see a neurologist."

"A virus? Guillain-Barré?" Holly guessed.

"Maybe." He hoped not, but knew it was a possibility. Guillain-Barré certainly wasn't fatal, but it was a progressive disease that often got worse before it got better. Patients usually recovered fully.

Thank heavens his mother was here to help.

"Are you in the mood for some company?" he asked, trying not to betray how badly he wanted to see her.

There was a pause and his heart dropped.

"Yes. I'd love some company," she finally said.

He sighed in relief. "Great. I was hoping you hadn't changed your mind."

The sound of her laugh reassured him. "No way. I've been waiting for you to call."

She'd been waiting for him. The thought sent a shaft of desire straight to his groin. "I'm on my way."

He hung up the phone and barely said goodbye to his mother before dashing out to his car.

There was no reason for Holly to wait any longer.

Holly flung clothes out of her closet, trying to find something classy yet sexy to wear.

Why didn't she own a single item of clothing that made her feel sexy without being too obvious? Finally settling on a V-necked ruby-red sweater and a pair of black jeans, she barely had time to hide the mess in her closet when the doorbell rang.

Taking a deep breath to calm her jagged nerves, Holly swiped her damp palms down the sides of her jeans and forced herself to walk slowly to the door. When she saw Gabe standing there, looking anxious, her nervousness faded.

She opened the door with a shy smile. "Hi."

"Hi." Holding a slender brown paper bag in the crook of his arm, Gabe stepped inside, bringing a cool gust of autumn air. "I brought wine."

"Great." She took the bottle of wine so he could shrug out of his leather jacket. Wearing black jeans and a white shirt, open at the throat, he looked wonderful.

She must have been gawking because he smiled as he reached for the wine. "I think I remember where your corkscrew is."

Following him to the kitchen, she remembered the last time he'd arrived on her doorstep, just a few nights ago. Back then she'd been running from her feelings.

She wasn't running from them tonight.

The air crackled with tension as Gabe opened the wine and poured two glasses. Carrying them both in one hand, he drew her to the sofa, urging her to sit before handing her one of the glasses.

"Here's to us," he offered as a toast. "To the beginning of something special."

Something special? Her throat went dry and she couldn't speak as she took a sip of the fruity red wine. Did that mean what she thought it meant?

"Holly." Gabe reached up to cradle her cheek in the palm of his hand. "You're so beautiful. I thought of you all day."

She wanted to tell him to stop, that he didn't have to say nice things because she already wanted him. More than she'd ever wanted any man.

Even Tom. Especially Tom.

"Gabe," she murmured, not sure of how to tell him, to express what she really wanted. And then she didn't have to. Because he read her mind, taking her wineglass from her fingers and drawing her into his arms for a deep kiss.

Yes. This was what she wanted. Gabe's warm strength surrounding her, his mouth taking possession of hers. Reaching up she entwined her arms around his neck, pulling him closer against her. In a deft movement he lifted her up, pressing her back against the couch so she was stretched out beneath him.

She reveled in the hard length of him pressing against her. He was strength and tenderness wrapped in one desirable male package. Gabe raised his head, his eyes desperate with need as he gazed down at her.

"Holly, please, tell me you want this as much as I do." His husky admission only fueled her passion. No man had ever looked at her with such desire.

"Yes, Gabe. I want this as much as you do." She swallowed hard and admitted, "Maybe more."

CHAPTER NINE

GABE stared at her for a long moment. He was almost afraid to believe he'd heard right.

"Please, be sure," he murmured hoarsely. Every muscle in his body was taut with need. Never in his life had he wanted a woman as much as he wanted Holly.

Her smile was seductive, sensual and she reached up to thread her fingers through his hair. "I'm sure. Kiss me, Gabe."

Gladly. He'd kiss her all day, every day, given the chance. Holding his weight off her with one arm, he leaned down to cover her mouth with his.

Her sofa didn't provide a lot of room, but as far as he was concerned they weren't in a hurry either. He kissed her slowly but deeply, enjoying the wine-tinged taste of her mouth and the feel of her soft breasts pressed against him. He wanted to strip their clothing away, to see every creamy inch of her skin, but he held himself in control.

Barely.

Holly tugged on his shirt, sliding her hands underneath the fabric, her hands cool against his fevered skin.

Shifting his weight off her as much as he could, he trailed a path of kisses to her throat. And then as far down as her V-necked sweater would let him go.

"My bedroom," she gasped, as he nudged the fabric aside and found the upper curve of her breast.

"In a minute," he whispered, pushing her sweater up and out of the way. He took a moment to admire the way her breasts looked in the lacy blue bra before making quick work of the front clasp.

A guy had to like expensive lingerie. Some things were worth any price.

Gently peeling the bra away, he freed her breasts. Annoyed with his own shirt, he ripped it off and then gathered her close, enjoying the feeling of her softness against him.

Holly ran her fingers over his back, making him shiver. He loved the way she touched him, full of awe and wonder.

"Did you say something about your bedroom?" he asked, lightly brushing a kiss over her mouth.

"Did I?" Her eyes were glazed with passion. "Oh, yes, down the hall."

Down the hall seemed like miles, yet as much as he didn't want to move he knew Holly deserved to be comfortable.

He wanted this night to be special for her. JT was in good hands with his grandmother. He didn't want to feel guilty for stealing these few hours alone.

Tonight was for Holly. And for him.

Peeling himself away from her, he held on to one of

her hands as he stood, bringing her up beside him, un-willing to let her go, even for a moment. He didn't bother trying to find his discarded shirt but led the way down the hall, figuring out which bedroom was hers by a process of elimination.

He didn't flip on the light switch as he entered the room, wanting to see her but not willing to make her feel self-conscious.

It took a few seconds for his eyes to adjust to the darkness. There was a little bit of light shining through the doorway, enough that he could make out the large bed in the center of the room. He paused at the edge of her bed and turned to face her.

"There's still time to change your mind," he felt obligated to point out, although he hoped and prayed she wouldn't.

She didn't answer, but grasped the hem of her sweater and lifted it up and over her head. Her open bra fell off her slim shoulders to the floor. When she stepped forward and reached for the fly of his jeans, he groaned and tried to hang on to the last vestiges of his control.

Her fingers seemed to spend more time exploring him than getting rid of his clothes. When he couldn't take her exquisite torture a moment longer, he shucked his jeans and boxers in a swift motion, and then reached for her. Lifting her up, he gently placed her on the bed, and then he peeled off her jeans and matching blue bikini underwear.

Damn, she was beautiful. He wished the lights were on so he could explore every inch of her satiny skin, but there wasn't time. Holly was already urgently reaching for him, her deft hands igniting small fires as they touched him everywhere.

"Please, Gabe…"

He couldn't deny her, not when his pleasure depended on hers. He fished in his jeans for protection, and then returned the favor, stroking her skin, kissing her breasts until he could barely think. When she wrapped her legs around his hips he couldn't hold off another moment, but slid deep, branding her as his.

The strong feeling of possessiveness shocked him. As he made love to Holly, drawing out the sensation until they both reached the pinnacle of pleasure, he held her close, burying his face in her hair, knowing things had irrevocably changed.

She belonged to him now. And he wasn't planning to ever let her go.

Holly held on to Gabe's strong shoulders, her face pressed to the hollow of his neck, deeply shaken by the experience they'd shared.

Gabe was a wonderful lover. Unselfish to the core, seeking to satisfy her needs before his own. Even after he shifted to the side, he gathered her close as if unable to bear leaving any space between them.

She closed her eyes, relaxing against him, enjoying the moment for as long as it lasted. He'd probably have to leave soon. She understood he wouldn't be able to stay the night.

JT needed him.

A tiny part of her mind realized Gabe must have felt better about leaving JT with his grandmother than with a babysitter, even someone as responsible as Marybeth.

But what would happen when Marybeth was released by the doctor to return to her babysitting duties and JT's grandmother went home?

The tumultuous thought wouldn't leave her alone, even though she knew she was borrowing trouble.

Best not to worry so much about the future. Gabe had claimed they needed to take things slow. Making love with him hadn't exactly been slowly, but she figured he was really referring to her relationship with JT. That was the part they needed to take slow.

Not this part. The being-with-him-in-her-bed part.

Gabe didn't leave. Several hours later he woke her up, making love to her again, this time languidly exploring her body as if they had all the time in the world.

Eventually, she realized how late it had become. Dawn was just an hour or two away.

She fell asleep again, waking up only when Gabe kissed her. "I have to go to work," he whispered.

"Okay," she murmured groggily.

"I'm going to borrow your shower."

She nodded, yawned and stretched while Gabe disappeared into her bathroom. Her alarm wouldn't go off for another half-hour, but she climbed out of bed anyway, to make Gabe some coffee before he left. Seemed like the least she could do after the wonderful night they'd shared.

She pulled her robe on and padded to the kitchen. Did Gabe eat breakfast? She wasn't sure. Truthfully there was a lot she still didn't know about him.

Although she already knew the important stuff. Like what a great lover he was. And what a wonderful, unselfish father he was to JT. Family was important to him, too.

He'd spent the whole night with her. Somehow she hadn't expected he'd do that, even with his mother at his house, watching over JT.

Gabe walked into the kitchen fully dressed in the clothes he'd worn last night. "Good morning," he said huskily, pulling her close for a kiss.

"Good morning." She was breathless when he finally let her go. As he reached for his mug of coffee, his cellphone rang.

Gabe frowned as he pulled open his phone. "Hi, Mom. What's up?"

His face paled and his expression turned grim as he listened on the other end of the phone. "I'll meet you at the hospital," he said in a terse tone.

The hospital? "Gabe? What's wrong?"

"She called 911 for an ambulance because JT's having seizures. I need to go."

She could only watch as he spun on his heel, grabbed his coat and bolted out the door.

He never should have gone to Holly's house last night.

He never should have left JT alone.

He'd never be a good father.

The self-recriminations echoed over and over in his

mind as he barreled through the streets of Minneapolis, cutting the normally short drive to the hospital in half.

How long had JT been having seizures? All night? His gut clenched with pain. What if JT suffered irreversible neurological damage as a result?

Guilt swelled, choking him. Dear God, JT had to be all right. He just had to be.

Gabe beat the ambulance to the hospital. He paced the center of the ED arena but then belatedly realized he was scheduled to work. Inwardly swearing, he headed off to find Mike Johnson, the physician who'd staffed the ED overnight.

He found Mike sitting in front of one of the bedside computers, finishing his chart documentation, and quickly explained what had happened with JT.

"Hey, it's all right," Mike said in his normal, easy-going manner. "I'll stay and make a few phone calls to find someone to cover your shift."

Gabe was grateful his colleague was so willing to help out. "Thanks." He glanced down, realizing his hands were shaking.

What was taking the ambulance so long to get here? Had something happened to JT on the way? His mind easily painted the worst picture, imagining the paramedic team running a full-blown respiratory and cardiac resuscitation on JT during the trip to the hospital.

Then suddenly he saw JT's name listed on the arena's census board. The doors from the ambulance bay burst open and a team of paramedics wheeled JT in, his mother hurrying alongside.

"What happened on the way?" Gabe asked, gazing down at JT, who appeared to be asleep. No breathing tube had been placed, thank heavens. But clearly the boy wasn't very responsive to his surroundings.

"We gave him a dose of Versed and the seizures stopped. But he's still pretty lethargic. His vital signs are stable, except he's running a fairly high fever—102.8 Fahrenheit."

Had the fever caused the seizure? "Get him on the monitor and then draw a full set of labs, including blood cultures. We also need a chest X ray."

The nursing staff stepped up to take over JT's care from the paramedic team that had brought him in. Gabe stared at JT's peaceful face, wondering what was going on in the boy's small body. A virus of some sort was the obvious answer, but what kind? And if it was Guillain-Barré syndrome, that didn't typically cause seizures or a high fever.

"Get a neurology consult, too," he added, remembering the pediatrician's recommendation. "And I want a CT scan of his head."

Someone tapped him on the arm. "I'm officially taking over as the physician of record here, Gabe."

He glanced down to see Dr. Tara Irwin standing beside him. Mike must have called her to cover his shift. While he was grateful, he was also a little annoyed. His feelings must have shown on his face.

"Don't argue with me, Gabe," she warned.

At her determined expression, his annoyance faded. He stepped back, knowing Tara was absolutely right.

He couldn't be calm and rational, not when JT's life was at stake.

Especially when they didn't even know what was wrong with him.

He listened as Tara confirmed most of his orders and added a few of her own, including an infectious disease consult. JT woke up, crying a little when a nurse drew blood.

"Shh, it's okay, buddy." Gabe pulled a chair close to JT's bed, taking his hand. "I'm here. I love you, JT."

Shortly after they finished the procedure, JT fell asleep again. Gabe tried not to panic at the extent of his lethargy, as it was normal after a seizure.

As the staff hurried to complete the orders, his mother came up to stand beside him. "Are you all right?" she asked.

"Fine." His words were clipped and he realized he was coming across as angry. And he was mad, but at himself, not at his mother. He'd made the decision to leave JT in her care while he went to Holly's. This was his fault and no one else's. "Sorry, I'm just worried about him."

"I know." His mother laid a hand on his shoulder. "But stop beating yourself up, Gabe. JT was fine last night, I checked on him before I went to bed. This morning I heard him cry out as if he was having a nightmare so I hurried into his room. His body started to convulse, on the right side especially, so I quickly called 911 and then called you."

Gabe closed his eyes, relieved to know JT hadn't been seizing all night.

"Thanks for telling me," he said finally. Maybe she was right, and nothing would have changed even if he had been there. Was it so wrong to take some time for himself? He didn't really think so yet, no matter how illogical, he couldn't get past the feeling he'd let JT down.

Maybe he wasn't cut out to be a father.

"Dr. Martin?" One of the nurses poked her head into the room. "Radiology called to tell us they're ready for JT. We're going to take him over for his CT scan now."

"All right." Gabe stood and moved back, so the transport team of the nurse and the radiology aide could disconnect JT from the heart monitor. Gabe watched, bereft, as they wheeled his son away.

"Are you hungry?" his mother asked.

He shook his head, knowing he couldn't eat. "Go ahead, though. I'll just wait here for JT to get back." CT scans of the head didn't take long.

His mother seemed to hesitate, but then nodded. "All right, I'll be back in a little while."

He sat back in the chair, cradling his head in his hands. JT had to be all right. They'd figure out what was wrong with him and they'd treat him. He'd be fine.

He had to believe JT would be fine.

"Gabe?"

He raised his head at the sound of Holly's voice. She stood in the doorway, as if unsure of her welcome.

For a moment he longed to go to her, to take her into his arms, drawing comfort. But he couldn't move. As much as he knew that none of this was her fault, he couldn't get past how he'd selfishly gone over to her house, leaving JT home alone with his grandmother.

"Where's JT?" she asked, taking another step farther into the room. "How is he?"

"They stopped the seizure but he's still pretty out of it." Gabe strove to keep his tone steady, although inside he felt as if he might shatter into a dozen little pieces. "He's in Radiology for a CT of his head."

"I see." Holly's expression was wary, as if she could sense how he regretted the time they'd spent together. None of this was her fault either. She hadn't asked him to spend the night.

He'd made that decision on his own.

"Thanks for coming to see him," he said.

She licked her lips and glanced away. "Actually, I'm here on consult."

That's right, he remembered Tara requesting an infectious disease consult. He tried to pull his scattered thoughts together. To see Holly as a physician, not as the woman he'd spent the night making love with. "Do you think he could have viral meningitis?" he asked.

Holly shook her head. "I checked the results of the LP they did on JT yesterday—there's no evidence of meningitis."

Gabe sighed, unsure if that was good news. At least if they had a diagnosis they could formulate a treatment plan. "He was running a fever this morning. It could be that the seizure was related to the fever and not to anything neurological."

"Maybe." Holly didn't sound convinced.

Their conversation was interrupted when the nurse brought JT back to his room. Once he was reconnected to the bedside monitor, Holly came forward.

"I'll need to examine him."

Gabe stood back, allowing Holly to do her job. He felt sick all over again when he realized JT was still pretty lethargic. If JT's responsiveness didn't improve, he'd end up getting intubated in order to protect his airway. Remembering Mark's mother's traumatic reaction to watching her son be intubated, he suddenly understood exactly how she'd felt.

Swallowing hard, he watched Holly go through her in-depth exam. When she'd finished, she turned toward him.

"Has JT always been afraid of wild animals?" she asked.

"No." He didn't understand what she was getting at.

She hesitated, then said, "I think we should test him for rabies."

Rabies? Gabe stared at her. "Why? There's no way JT could have been exposed to rabies."

"Yesterday morning, JT told me wild animals bite. Then he said he saw a raccoon at the cemetery, and I'm assuming that was probably during Claire's funeral." When he nodded, she continued, "Four to six weeks is the typical incubation period for rabies. What if he saw a rabid raccoon and it bit him? I don't want to ignore any possibilities."

Gabe had trouble wrapping his mind around the implications. "But he hasn't been given the vaccination for rabies."

Holly didn't say anything. She didn't have to. Once a patient showed clinical signs of rabies, the mortality rate was very high.

The tightness in his chest intensified. If JT had really been exposed to rabies six weeks ago, there was a very good chance he would die.

CHAPTER TEN

HOLLY cradled the phone receiver between her ear and her shoulder, listening to the dreadful music as she waited for the lab tech at the Center for Disease Control to put her in touch with the physician who specialized in rabies. As soon as Gabe had admitted there was a possibility JT had been bitten by a raccoon, she'd called to get their recommendations.

Rabies wasn't very common. Treatment after known rabies contact had become so good there had been little recent research on the subject. Local labs didn't even run tests for rabies. If infection was suspected, the patient was simply treated no matter what any blood tests showed.

"Dr. Davidson? This is Dr. Lois Whitney at the CDC. I was told you have a case of suspected rabies?"

"Yes." Holly explained the potential raccoon bite and then described JT's symptoms. She'd noticed JT's right side was convulsing and he was salivating more than normal, which was one of the symptoms of rabies. In reading up on the disease, she'd discovered some patients had literally drowned in their own secretions.

"Send us some blood and cerebral spinal fluid samples immediately," Dr. Whitney told her. "Put them on dry ice and ship them as fast as possible." Lois Whitney hesitated, and then added, "From what you described, you'd better treat him as if he is positive for rabies."

"I understand." Holly hung up the phone, feeling sick. She'd hoped she'd been wrong about JT having contracted rabies.

Without immediate post-exposure vaccinations, the disease was highly fatal.

She took several deep breaths, trying to hold panic at bay. They had the best medical experts in the country here at the Children's Medical Center. If anyone could get JT through this, they could.

Poor Gabe. She knew how devastated she'd been after losing Kayla. Losing JT would be worse. Much worse.

Stop it. She mentally gave herself a hard shake. They weren't going to lose him.

Somehow they were going to find a way to successfully treat him.

Turning blindly from the desk, she bumped into Dr. Jeff Konen, the neuro specialist assigned to JT's case. He'd come in to examine JT right after she'd broached the possibility of rabies.

"According to the CDC, we need to treat JT Martin as if he has rabies. And we need to get some blood and cerebral spinal fluid samples sent to Atlanta immediately."

The older man blew out a heavy breath. "Okay, so if your theory is correct and he was bitten almost six weeks ago, then the virus has already begun its attack on his central nervous system. The typical rabies vaccine injections are used to prevent the virus from attacking the nervous system. In JT's case, it's too late to prevent that. Which means we have to try to minimize the damage."

The large knot in her stomach tightened. She knew the mechanism of disease as well as he did. This long after the time of infection, there wasn't much that could be done to stop the progression of the virus.

"We need to talk to Gabe, to include him in this discussion," she said firmly. Gabe was a physician as well as being JT's uncle. He'd want to be included in all aspects of JT's care.

Jeff hesitated and nodded, turning toward JT's room. She followed close behind.

While she'd been in touch with the CDC, the nurses had placed JT in isolation. Both she and Jeff donned a face mask, gown and gloves before entering the room.

Gabe wasn't wearing any isolation gear, as if he could care less if he was contaminated by the virus. From her research she knew that person-to-person transmission of the virus was rare. Still, infectious disease literature said that it was better to be safe by placing patients in isolation.

Gabe sat on JT's bed, holding the boy in his arms. His face was pale and drawn, his eyes bleak with grief.

"The CDC would like samples of JT's blood and cerebral spinal fluid," she told him. "They recommended we treat JT as if he's already tested positive for rabies."

Gabe gave a slight nod. She wasn't sure if he was

agreeing to send blood to the CDC or to the proposed treatment plan. Hopefully both.

Jeff stepped forward. "Gabe, I propose we get JT intubated and sent up to the PICU. I think if we paralyze and sedate him, putting him into a barbiturate coma, we'll have a chance to protect his brain while it fights the virus."

Holly raised a brow. The neurologist's proposal was intriguing. And somewhat experimental. Similar treatment plans had been tried but not all of them had been successful. There were so many variables, especially as there were at least eleven different strains of the rabies virus.

When Gabe didn't say anything right away, she spoke up. "Gabe, I've done some research on rabies, and there has been limited success with this approach. I have to agree with Jeff's treatment plan. I'd also add another possibility. Ketamine, a drug used primarily for anesthesia, has been shown to decrease the rabies virus in mice. It hasn't been tested on humans, but if we use a combination of ketamine and Versed to decrease the toxic effects on JT's brain, we may have a chance to beat the virus."

There were no guarantees. As a physician Gabe had to understand that more than anyone. Yet Holly firmly believed that if doctors did not try, they would not succeed. If the chances were high that JT might die, there was no reason not to try this radical treatment option.

Gabe gazed so intently down at JT she wondered if he'd heard anything they'd said. But then he slowly nodded.

"Do whatever you have to do to save my son."

His son. Tears burned the back of her eyes and she had to look away, biting her lip behind the face mask.

Once they had paralyzed and sedated JT, they could ensure he wouldn't feel any more pain or discomfort.

Gabe's suffering, for the son he might never get to formally adopt, would be much harder to bear.

Gabe didn't leave JT's bedside except to eat and to use the bathroom. Eating wasn't exactly high on his priority list. He wasn't hungry but knew he needed to keep up his strength, in order to support JT.

His mother insisted on staying in Minneapolis, despite the fact that he encouraged her to go home to her husband. Clearly he no longer needed her to watch JT while he was at work.

There was no reason for her to sit here with him. JT's recovery would likely take weeks. Maybe even months.

He refused to consider the alternative. The physician part of him understood the risks, but as a parent he chose to ignore them.

JT would pull through this. He'd make sure of it.

The hours merged into days. He lost track of time, sleeping on the parent bed next to JT in the PICU.

He couldn't complain about JT's care. Everyone bent over backward to take excellent care of his son. Within twenty-four hours of sending blood and cerebral spinal fluid samples to Atlanta, the CDC had confirmed the diagnosis of rabies.

Holly had been right after all.

He couldn't hold JT in his lap anymore now that he was intubated and breathing with the help of a ventilator. There were so many tubes and wires in JT he was almost afraid to touch him. All JT's nutrition came through a feeding tube, not to mention myriad IV medications he was receiving. He knew that despite the radical combination of medications Jeff and Holly had ordered for JT, it was possible the treatments might not work.

So he prayed, like he'd never prayed before.

On Friday, his mother came into JT's room with a pile of mail she'd brought from his house. Gabe hadn't been home since meeting JT and his mother at the hospital, and he found it difficult to care about mundane things like phone bills and bank statements.

One of the letters snagged his attention because it was from the DNA lab in the Minnesota State Lab in Minneapolis. He stared at the envelope for a long time. The DNA results declaring the identity of JT's biological father were inside. This was what he'd been waiting for, in order to move forward with JT's adoption.

He almost threw the envelope away. JT's life hung in the balance—what difference did it make who his biological father was?

Except that maybe JT's biological father deserved to know the truth. Especially now that JT was so sick.

Especially when there was a possibility JT might not survive.

He stared at the letter for a long time, struggling with what to do. If the situation were reversed and he'd fathered a child that no one had told him about, he'd want to know the truth.

"Gabe? Are you all right?" his mother asked.

"Yeah, I'm fine." He opened the letter and scanned the results. Rising to his feet, he glanced down at JT, still motionless in the barbiturate coma. He knew what he had to do. "Will you stay here with JT for a few minutes?"

His mother glanced at him in surprise. "Of course I will."

Gabe nodded and left the room, pulling his cellphone out of his pocket. Then he swore when he realized the battery was dead. He hadn't recharged his phone over the past few days.

He turned and headed to the PICU waiting room. There was a phone in there he could use. If the operator would give him an outside line.

He had a long-distance phone call to make.

Holly checked on JT and Gabe as often as her schedule allowed. Sometimes she came and sat with him at the end of the day, but Gabe didn't say much.

She knew he blamed himself for the seriousness of JT's illness. And maybe a small part of him blamed her as well.

What could she say? There were no words to make him feel better. They were doing everything possible to save JT's life.

All they could do was wait.

On Friday evening she headed into the PICU to find Gabe walking out from the waiting room. She was surprised to see him outside the PICU when he'd been practically living at JT's bedside.

"Hey," he greeted her weakly.

"Hi, Gabe." She longed to put her arms around him, to hold him close. Sometimes she wondered if she'd imagined those stolen hours they'd spent together at her house the night before JT had become so sick. The only evidence she had to prove it wasn't her imagination was the fact that her sheets still carried a hint of Gabe's musky scent.

Gabe stared at her for a long moment, before glancing away. "I need to thank you," he said slowly. "If you hadn't brought up the possibility of rabies when you did, it would have been too late."

She hoped it wasn't too late. So far, she knew JT's vital signs were good, but they wouldn't know about his level of brain function until they brought him out of the coma.

"You don't have to thank me. I wish there was more I could do. I care about you, Gabe. I care about both of you."

"I know." At that moment his stoic expression cracked, revealing the vulnerable man beneath. Unable to ignore his pain, she closed the gap between them and wrapped her arms around his waist, determined to offer comfort even if he did push her away.

He didn't.

Instead, his arms came up to crush her close, his face buried in her hair as he murmured, "I can't lose him, Holly. I just can't."

"I know." She battled tears, holding on to him tightly. She wasn't one to offer false hope but in this case they needed to think positively. "You won't. I'll be here for you. We have to believe you won't lose him."

"I've been a lousy father so far," Gabe whispered.

What? She pulled back to look into his eyes. "That's not true. Compared to Tom, you've been wonderful. Stop blaming yourself, Gabe. How could you know JT had been bitten by a raccoon? The bite would have been so small it was barely noticeable. And how could you know that the raccoon carried rabies?"

"I don't know. I just don't want to lose him." The self-reproach in his eyes made her draw him close, give him another tight hug. His grip tightened, too, as if he needed the support as much as she needed to give it.

She held Gabe for a long time, offering him a little of her strength. When he finally lifted his head and loosened his arms, he brushed a light kiss over her mouth, as if offering silent thanks. "I know you're scheduled to work this weekend, but will you stay, at least for a little while?"

Thrilled and humbled that he'd realized he couldn't do this alone without help and support, she nodded. "Of course. I'll stay for as long as you need me."

"Thanks." Gabe took a deep breath and let it out slowly. He offered a crooked smile and held out his hand. "Let's go."

She took his hand and walked with him into the PICU. Their clasped hands drew a couple of curious glances from the PICU nurses but Holly couldn't bring herself to care. What did a few whispers matter in the big scheme of things?

The only thing that mattered was the fact that Gabe and JT needed her. And if she was honest, she needed them too.

Gabe's mother greeted her with a wide smile. She got the distinct impression his mother approved of Holly's new yet tenuous relationship with her son.

That night, Holly stretched out next to Gabe on the narrow parent bed in JT's room. He held her close, her head resting on his shoulder, their embrace cozily intimate despite the fact that they were both fully clothed. Gabe had changed into a pair of comfortable sweats and a T-shirt, while she'd borrowed a pair of scrubs to wear.

Still, Holly was poignantly aware of the message her actions sent to anyone who walked into the room to care for JT.

She and Gabe were a couple. Together they were supporting JT and each other.

She loved him. The shocking realization made her eyes fly open. Her chest felt tight, as if she couldn't breathe.

Love? How could this have happened? For a moment panic swelled as she stared blindly at the tile ceiling. Falling in love usually meant getting married. Having a family. Another child, hers and Gabe's.

Could she have a family of her own? There was a tiny part of her that always thought she'd feel disloyal to Kayla if she had another child.

Yet being here, next to JT's bedside while the boy fought for his life, she slowly realized nothing could be further from the truth.

Having Kayla had taught her to love. Loving one person didn't mean you couldn't love another. JT needed all the love and support he could get.

So did Gabe.

Nothing else mattered.

The next morning, she awoke when Jeff Konen came into the room. Groggily, she swung her legs over the side of the bed, sitting next to Gabe who'd also just woken up. Jeff eyed her presence beside Gabe curiously, but didn't comment.

"How long do we need to keep JT in a coma?" Gabe asked, scrubbing a hand over his face.

"I'm not sure," Jeff admitted. He glanced at Holly. "What do you think?"

Holly blinked and forced herself to focus. "A full week, to be safe."

Jeff nodded. "Yeah, that's what I was thinking too. We'll start tapering off the medications early next week."

"So there's nothing more to do at this point but to wait," Gabe said.

"I'm afraid so," Jeff admitted.

Waiting was difficult. Holly knew where Gabe was coming from. As a physician he was accustomed to action. Not to the wait-and-see approach.

After Jeff left the room, Holly slowly rose to her feet. "I have to get ready for work," she said, wishing she didn't have to leave.

Gabe nodded, watching her as she gathered her things together. It was too late to run home for a change of clothes so she decided to find a call room to shower and change into a fresh set of scrubs. Scrubs paired with a lab coat would have to do.

"Thanks for staying," Gabe said in a low voice.

She gave him another hug, knowing they'd need to talk but that this wasn't the time. Not when JT's fate was still largely unknown. "I'll be back tonight, unless you decide you don't want me here."

Gabe reached up to cup the side of her face. "I do want you here," he murmured, before bending his head down to kiss her.

His kiss was brief but potent. Her senses swam as she momentarily lost herself in his embrace. He broke off the kiss when one of JT's nurses entered the room.

Holly stepped back, feeling a little self-conscious but not to the point where she regretted one second of their embrace. "I'll see you later," she promised, before picking up her clothes and leaving the room.

Holly showered and changed before starting her rounds. Each of the infectious disease doctors had to take turns staffing on the weekends. She didn't mind, but, having had much of her sleep broken during the night with interruptions from the nurses caring for JT, she had to battle her fatigue with several strong cups of coffee.

She came through the PICU to check on JT halfway through the day. Gabe was still there and he greeted her with a smile that warmed her heart. She was amazed that he was holding up as well as he was.

"I'm going to run home after work but then I'll be back," she told him.

"Thanks, Holly. I appreciate it."

She honestly didn't mind. In fact, she finished her rounds on the floors sooner than she'd expected and as there were no new consults called in she was able to leave by three in the afternoon.

She changed into comfortable clothes, debating what to bring back to the hospital with her. Because if Gabe wanted her to spend the night with him again, she would. Gladly.

In the end she decided to bring enough clothes for the rest of the weekend. She had to work on Monday too, but by then they might have started weaning JT from his medications. They couldn't take him out of the coma too quickly, but would need to take their time over several days.

She didn't eat dinner, deciding she'd force Gabe to eat with her, knowing he probably wasn't taking care of himself the way he should. Arriving back at the hospital, she felt self-conscious bringing an overnight bag into the PICU.

Entering JT's room, she halted when she realized Gabe wasn't alone.

Tom was standing there, gazing down at JT. She frowned, trying to figure out why her ex-husband was there. Had Gabe called him, seeking support from his former best friend?

"Holly." Gabe's expression was pained when he saw her standing there. "Come in. Ah—you know Tom of course."

Of course. What she didn't know was what Tom was doing there. Something was wrong, she could feel it in the somber atmosphere in the room. Her stomach twisted painfully. Had JT taken a turn for the worse? "Hi, Tom. Gabe, is something wrong?"

"No, nothing is wrong." Gabe's expression held a note of uncertainty. "I guess I should explain. Holly, you need to know I called Tom because I felt he deserved to be here, to see JT for himself."

She didn't understand. "Deserved to be here?"

"Yes." Gabe's gaze was apologetic. "I hate having to tell you like this but DNA results have confirmed Tom is JT's biological father."

CHAPTER ELEVEN

HOLLY stared at Gabe in horror. Tom? JT's father? From somewhere beside her she heard a nurse gasp, and when she realized they had an audience, her face flamed red with acute embarrassment.

Why did things like this always happen to her when other people were around to witness her humiliation?

Gabe's words ricocheted through her mind, over and over, like a bad dream. Tom Richards was JT's biological father. JT was five years old. Her ex-husband must have had an affair with Claire.

Before their wedding.

She took one step back. Then another. Gabe moved toward her but she held up a hand, warding him off. "Don't."

He halted, his gaze full of compassion. A part of her wanted to go to him for comfort yet at the same time she couldn't get past the fact he'd lied to her. Or at the very least withheld the truth from her.

Had Gabe known about the affair even back then? Had he known about Tom and Claire but had chosen not to say anything to her? Why? For what purpose? To protect Tom?

Even back then she'd thought Gabe had been her friend too, not just Tom's.

Gabe had walked out on the wedding. All these years she'd assumed it had been because of her attempt to kiss him, crossing the line of friendship. But maybe it was really because he'd found out about the affair.

And he hadn't told her.

Unable to tolerate being there a moment longer, she spun on her heel and bolted from the room, nearly barreling into the surprised nurse who stood in the doorway.

Blindly she made her way through the hospital to the parking structure. She found her car, belatedly realizing she'd left her overnight case in JT's room. She climbed into the driver's seat, blinking away her tears.

Gabe had lied to her. She couldn't get past the pain of knowing that she'd given him her trust but he'd still lied to her.

Just like Tom had lied to her.

Only Gabe's betrayal was worse. Much worse.

Because even in this short period of time she'd come to depend on Gabe to keep his word. Tom had often said things but had never followed through on them. But Gabe was different. Or so she'd thought.

She loved JT like a son. And now she had to accept the fact that her ex-husband was JT's biological father. Every time she looked at JT, she'd be reminded about Tom's infidelity.

Infidelity that had begun before the wedding. Infidelity that had lasted throughout their short marriage.

Her stomach lurched and she swallowed hard, fighting nausea, leaning forward to rest her head on the steering wheel. She didn't care about Tom, not anymore, but obviously she didn't have the relationship she'd thought she had with Gabe.

She'd fallen in love with Gabe. With JT.

But Gabe had lied to her.

How could she ever trust him again?

Gabe swore inwardly, as Holly ran from the PICU. Damn, he'd handled that badly. Yet logically he knew he couldn't change the facts.

Tom was JT's father.

And he still planned to adopt JT. But he couldn't blame Holly for being upset and angry. How could she have a relationship with him, knowing that if their relationship progressed to something serious, it was possible she'd help raise her ex-husband's bastard son?

He scrubbed his hands over his face, feeling as if he stood on the edge of a cliff, the ground crumbling beneath his feet.

He needed to step back, to get grounded and focus on what was important.

He may have lost Holly but JT needed him. There was a chance the young boy might not make it. The five-year-old was lying in an ICU bed, his body functioning only with the help of machines. So far, Gabe had held on to hope but until the team of doctors, including Holly, brought JT out of his coma, they wouldn't know if their experimental treatment had worked.

JT could end up with severe brain damage. The little boy he had been might cease to exist.

"Gabe, you know I'll sign the paperwork," Tom said from beside him.

It took him a moment to realize what Tom was talking about. The adoption paperwork they'd been discussing before Holly had walked in. Tom was willing to sign over his custodial rights, enabling Gabe to move forward with the adoption.

This was what he'd planed from the moment he'd learned Claire had died. Until the doubts had started to creep in.

But now he knew he'd do anything for JT. No matter what. He forced himself to nod. "Thanks. I already love JT like a son and he loves me. We're a good team."

They would be a better team with Holly.

He shied away from the painful thought.

Tom shifted to glance back at his son. "You're a better man than I am, Gabe. I don't think I could take care of him like you are. Kids really have a way of tying you down, you know?"

Tom was an idiot. Loving someone didn't tie you down. Love set you free. Love made you happy. But agreeing with Tom seemed rude. Although it was true. Gabe *was* a better man than he was.

"I'm sorry about Holly," Tom added.

Sorry for what? For cheating on her? For abandoning her when she'd needed him most? Gabe reined in his temper with an effort. "Holly deserves better, just like JT does."

"And that means you?" Tom asked, skepticism lacing his tone.

"Yes. Because I love her. A man who cheats on his wife while she's having a miscarriage doesn't know the meaning of the word."

Tom's eyebrows shot up. "So, she told you what happened, huh?" Tom shrugged. "I didn't mean to hurt her. I loved Holly in my own way. I don't know why I ended up seeing other women. I know you won't believe this but I really tried to be faithful. I actually almost told her the truth the night she told me she was pregnant. She was so happy I decided to keep my mouth shut. And then she miscarried."

Gabe's fingers curled into fists. Tom was right, he didn't really believe him. But, either way, it didn't matter. There was no justification for infidelity so he didn't bother to try to think of one. "Just sign the paperwork, will you? That's all I'm asking. I only called because I thought you'd want a chance to see your son." Before he died.

No, JT wasn't going to die. Not if he could help it.

"Sure. I'll sign." Tom took the legal document and signed the bottom by the X before handing it back to Gabe. Staring at Tom's signature, Gabe wondered if JT's illness had contributed to Tom's willingness to let him go. "I honestly hope JT makes it through this. No kid deserves to be this sick."

"He will," Gabe said with conviction.

"And good luck with Holly."

He didn't have a response to that. Because he'd seen the wounded devastation in her eyes. Luck alone wasn't going to help. He wasn't sure anything would.

After Tom had left, Gabe sat beside JT's bedside, cradling the child's hand in his.

Very soon it would be official. He'd become a father and JT would belong to him.

His chest tightened and he bowed his head. If only he hadn't lost Holly in the process.

The next morning Gabe waited for Holly to make rounds. She was too good a doctor to ignore one of her patients.

And JT was still her patient.

Her small overnight case was still sitting where she'd dropped it after discovering the shocking news that Tom was JT's biological father.

Gabe stared down at JT's small peaceful face, the breathing tube still in his lungs to allow the ventilator to do the work of breathing for him.

Waiting like this, not knowing if JT would survive, was so hard.

He already felt like a father. And loving someone, when you were helpless to fix them, was the most difficult thing to endure.

Holly came through at ten-thirty in the morning. Beneath her white lab coat she wore all black. A black turtleneck sweater tucked into trim black pants. Gabe couldn't help but wonder if she was wearing black for a reason, like mourning the end of a relationship that had barely begun.

Her face was pale and dark smudges underscored her brown eyes. Despite her obvious exhaustion, she still looked beautiful to him. He wanted to go to her but forced himself to stay where he was next to JT's bed.

She glanced at the clipboard in her hands. All the medical and nursing documentation was done in the bedside computer system, but Holly must have taken some notes. "We're planning to start tapering off his medications tomorrow morning."

Gabe nodded, understanding that it might take a while for JT to come out of the medication-induced coma. "Holly, I'm sorry you had to find out about Tom like that."

She avoided his gaze, lifting a shoulder in a helpless shrug. "No worse than watching him come out of his naked lover's call room."

He grimaced and jammed his fingers through his hair. "No, I guess not."

"It doesn't matter. I've been over Tom for a long time." Holly's tone was casual, as if she had more important things to worry about.

He doubted anyone could truly be over something like that, but if what she said was true, why was she acting so distant? So upset?

"Will you come back tonight, after your shift? We could go down to the cafeteria for dinner and talk." JT's condition had been relatively stable but Gabe was loath to leave the hospital just yet. He'd only gone home a couple of times to shower and change his clothes.

"No, I don't think so."

The knot deep in his belly tightened. "Why not?"

She let out a small sigh and finally brought her gaze to his. "Gabe, nothing changes the fact you lied to me."

"I didn't lie to you, Holly. I swear I didn't know who JT's biological father was until Friday." When he saw the skepticism in her eyes, he added, "You can see from his chart that JT's full name is John Tomas. Claire called him JT almost from the moment he was born. I found her personal journal after she died. She'd been intimate with two men, John Olsinksi and Tom. She didn't know which man had fathered JT so she christened him with both their names. I contacted both men, asking for DNA paternity tests."

"Why?"

He tried to make her understand. "Because the adoption agency asked if I knew who his biological father was and I explained it was likely to be one of the two men my sister had mentioned in her diary. The adoption agency suggested I get DNA samples to know for sure so that neither one of them could come back later with a parental claim once I adopted him."

"I see." Holly nodded slowly. "But I'm sure you must have known, even back then, that Tom was unfaithful."

"I suspected," he admitted slowly. "I didn't have proof, had never seen him so much as kiss another woman with my own eyes, but I suspected. The way he openly flirted with women, well, it just wasn't right."

Holly didn't respond.

"I'm sorry you were hurt, Holly. If I had known the truth I would have told you. Maybe I should have said something sooner, even without proof. Yet I have to be honest with you. At first I doubted my ability to do this, to be a parent to JT. But now I'm glad JT's father turned out to be a man willing to give up his rights to him." He didn't explain that John Olsinski had mentioned possibly taking custody of JT, if it turned out he was the father.

Now that Tom had signed, there was nothing standing in his way.

"I'm glad JT is going to be your son, Gabe," Holly said finally. "He needs a father like you."

"He needs more than just me," Gabe countered. This had been his worst fear, losing Holly once he knew for sure Tom was JT's father. Fighting to keep his voice steady, he said, "He needs a family."

Holly turned away. "The two of you with your mother, his grandmother, are a family. I'll be back to check on him tomorrow, after we start backing off on his medications."

He didn't want her to leave. Not like this. Not with so much left unsaid between them.

He loved her. He needed to tell her how much he loved her. How much he needed her support to get through this crisis with JT.

How much he needed her to believe in him, when he hadn't believed in himself.

But then he remembered Jennifer's unwillingness to raise JT as her own. Holly had a much better reason to be less than enthusiastic in raising JT as her own. Could he blame her for not wanting to live with the evidence of Tom's infidelity every day?

He didn't try to stop her when she walked away.

* * *

On Monday morning Holly entered the PICU eager to start doing something for JT besides simply waiting. She accessed the computer system and went into JT's chart, only to discover Jeff had beat her to it, having already written orders cutting the doses of his barbiturates, ketamine and Versed infusions in half.

A tiny thrill of anticipation shot through her. She and Jeff had discussed their strategy yesterday. First they'd cut the doses in half, and twelve hours later, if he didn't have any untoward side effects, they'd discontinue the medication completely.

And hopefully JT would start to wake up.

He wouldn't wake up right away, because it would take some time for his body to throw off the effects of the drugs. They'd kept him pretty deep in the coma, knowing he needed time and rest to keep his brain from succumbing to rabies toxicity.

She hoped their solution had worked.

After logging off the computer, she stood and warily approached JT's room. Gabe was there, as usual, seeming to be a permanent fixture at his son's bedside.

At the doorway, she hesitated, bracing herself to see him. Despite everything that had happened, once the initial sharp piercing pain had receded, she'd found herself thinking about him, replaying their conversation over and over again in her head.

There was a part of her that wanted to believe him. Wanted to believe he hadn't lied to her about the past and again now, more recently.

But trust didn't come easily. She knew Gabe and his

sister had been close. She found it hard to believe Claire hadn't confided in him, especially knowing she and Tom were to be married. And no matter what Gabe claimed, she knew he must have suspected that JT was really Tom's child.

She was finding it difficult to get over the fact he hadn't told her the minute he'd discovered the results. She'd spent the whole night with him, curled up beside him on the narrow cot beside JT.

Yet he still hadn't told her.

"Good morning." She kept her greeting polite as she entered the room. "I'm sure you realize by now that Jeff has cut all JT's medication doses in half."

Gabe smiled and nodded. "I wish they were off completely, but I guess we have to wait until later for that."

"Yes." She glanced up at the bedside monitor, frowning a little when she noticed JT's heart rate had jumped up. "How long has his heart rate been up like that?"

Gabe's smile faded. "Must have just happened because ten minutes ago it was hanging in the 118 range."

She tried not to show her worry, although this was exactly one of the problems she and Jeff had feared. That JT's body might react to the withdrawal of the medications. If so, they'd have to back off even more slowly.

"We may have to go back up on his medication," Holly warned. "I think we can give him a little time yet, but if his blood pressure drops, we'll have no choice but to back off."

Even as she spoke, JT's heart rate continued to climb. It started at 132 and pretty soon it was up to 140. When it hit 144 his blood pressure began to drop.

The PICU nurse rushed into the room. "What's wrong? Why is he having trouble?"

"We need to increase the medications again," Holly said. "Instead of cutting them in half, maybe we should have only cut them by a quarter."

The nurse adjusted the various IV pumps, putting the doses back up so that the drop wasn't so drastic.

Gabe didn't seem to notice she was there but continued to sit next to the bed, holding his son's hand. "Hang in there, JT. Please, hang in there. I need you, buddy. Please, come back."

Holly's throat swelled with emotion. No matter who had fathered JT biologically, she knew Gabe was his father in every way that counted.

She stared at the heart monitor, grateful that JT's pulse had stopped climbing. She took a moment, stepping out of the room in order to page Jeff Konen, to fill him in on the latest development. When she returned she was very glad to see that JT's blood pressure had come back up to within normal range.

Breathing a little easier, she watched his heart rate slowly drop. Not quite going all the way to normal, but at least it wasn't as high as it had been earlier. Jeff rushed into the room, staring at the monitor.

"He's better now," Holly said softly.

Jeff glanced at her. "So do we try to go back down on the medications in another six hours?"

She bit her lip, unsure. Each rabies case was so different there were no hard and fast rules.

"Yes," she finally said. "We should at least try.

Maybe he just needs time to allow his system to adjust to the new dose."

"Okay, I'll write the orders." Jeff left the room to find the nearest computer.

Holly pulled up a chair next to Gabe. JT wasn't out of the woods yet. His body might still reject the decreased medication levels.

She wasn't going to leave until she knew JT was stable.

CHAPTER TWELVE

FEELING completely helpless, Gabe watched JT's pulse and blood pressure fluctuate like a yo-yo.

Holly directed the nurse to make even smaller changes in the medication dosing. She hadn't left JT's bedside in hours. Gabe appreciated her dedication and support but was very afraid that at this rate JT wouldn't come out of his coma until Christmas.

If at all.

"Maybe he needs a longer time on the medication," Gabe said finally. "Maybe he's still suffering the effects of the virus and we're waking him up too soon."

"It's possible," Holly agreed, a troubled frown furrowing between her brows. "Although from all the case studies I've reviewed, a week from the onset of seizures should be enough time for the effects to resolve."

Gabe glanced at her. "And how many of those case studies discussed patients who were only five years old?"

"None." Holly let out a heavy sigh. "The youngest child was seven."

And the seven-year-old child had died. He knew

Holly didn't want to say the words but she didn't have to.

He'd reviewed much of the rabies literature himself, having read the same case studies she was referring to. He'd been impressed with the comprehensive treatment plan they'd adopted.

Yet all their attempts might be in vain.

He stared down at JT's tiny face, dwarfed by the breathing tube. How was it possible for one small boy to imbed himself so deeply into his heart in such a short time?

Granted, he'd known JT since his birth. Had tried to give Claire the extra bit of support she'd needed as a single mother. But being there for special events—birthdays and holidays—was as nothing compared to living with him day in and day out.

"JT has always been a climber," he murmured. "When he was just twelve months old I was watching him over at Claire's and I walked into his bedroom because it had been too quiet for too long, which always meant he was up to something. Sure enough, when I walked in I found him at eye level, standing on the top of his dresser. He nearly gave me a heart attack."

"How on earth did he get up there?" Holly asked.

"Used the open dresser drawers as rungs of a ladder." Gabe chuckled at the memory. "I was afraid to yell at him, I didn't want to startle him into falling, so I talked very nicely and quietly."

"He didn't fall, did he?"

"No." He shook his head wryly. "But I broke speed records getting from one side of the room to the other."

Unbidden, the memories kept coming. "Then there was the time he climbed to the top of the neighbor's swing set when he was barely two. And just a week ago he was telling me how he and his buddy climbed up to the loft during their trip to the dairy farm."

"Gabe." Holly put her hand on his arm. "Don't do this. He's going to pull through. I believe in my heart he's going to pull through this."

He momentarily closed his eyes against burning tears. "I hope so. I really hope so. I don't care if he doesn't climb anymore, I still want him to pull through this."

Holly's warm scent enveloped him when she put her arms around his shoulders for a comforting hug. He grabbed her and held on tight, needing her caring comfort more than he needed air to breathe.

She didn't say anything for a long time, simply held him. After what seemed like forever but was probably really only about twenty or thirty minutes, she loosened her grip.

"I need to call Jeff. I think we need a new strategy for JT," she said in a low tone. After instructing the nurse to stop all the medication titrations, she left the room.

Gabe felt Holly's absence like a sore tooth as he watched the monitor over JT's head, relieved to see his heart rate and blood pressure settle down a bit.

He owed her so much. She'd picked up on the rabies diagnosis very quickly, and had been working diligently ever since to save his son. Tom's son.

Her unselfishness was amazing.

* * *

By Wednesday morning Holly thought it was possible Gabe was right, that JT needed more time to allow the virus to work its way through his system.

"I think we should send more samples to the CDC," she told Jeff. "Maybe they can run some virus titers and let us know if we're making headway or not."

"All right," Jeff agreed. "Call your contact at the CDC and let them know we're sending more blood and cerebral spinal fluid samples."

"Sounds good." Holly hung up the phone and then wrote the orders in the computer. She was glad she didn't have to do the lumbar puncture on JT, she didn't think she could maintain her objectivity in order to get the task done.

When she'd finished the orders, she received a page from a number she didn't recognize. Frowning, she picked up the nearest phone.

"Outpatient Dialysis, this is Diane. May I help you?"

"Diane, this is Holly Davidson. Did someone page me?"

"Oh, yes, one of the nurses wanted to talk to you about your mother. Just a minute."

A wave of guilt hit her as Holly realized she hadn't kept in touch with her mother as often as she should have recently. Dealing with JT's illness had consumed a lot of her time.

And battling her feelings for Gabe had kept her pre-occupied as well. But none of that was her mother's fault.

What kind of daughter was she?

Apparently not a very good one.

The music abruptly cut off. "Hello, Holly? This is Angie, one of the dialysis nurses. I'm calling to let you know your mother is being transferred to Minneapolis Medical Center. She had a brief episode of cardiac arrest."

A brief episode of *cardiac arrest*? "What happened?"

"Her magnesium levels must have dropped, she went into a rhythm known as *torsades de pointes*, which is a type of V-fib normally treated with a bolus of magnesium. We were able to convert her very easily back into normal sinus rhythm, but felt she should be admitted to the hospital for evaluation."

Holly sucked in a deep breath and let it out slowly. She was very familiar with *torsades* and was grateful the nurses there had recognized the rhythm right away. Treatment was easy if you knew what you were looking at, but all too often *torsades* was missed. Good grief, she could just imagine how frightened her mother must be. "She's doing all right now?"

"Yes, her blood pressure is down a bit but we've given her a little albumin and she's coming up nicely." Dialysis patients couldn't be given very much fluid as their kidneys didn't work the same way a normal person's did.

"Tell her I'll meet her at the hospital," Holly instructed. "And tell her I love her."

"I will."

She made her call to the CDC, which took longer than she'd thought, and then spent another few minutes finishing her note in JT's chart. Afterwards, she went back into the boy's room to find Gabe.

He was right where she left him the day before,

seated in the chair next to JT's bed as if he'd become a permanent fixture in the room. She hesitantly approached the bedside. "Gabe? I just got off the phone with the CDC, and we're going to send more blood and spinal fluid samples from JT to Atlanta to see if he still has high levels of the virus. After those test results return, we'll have a better idea of how to proceed."

Gabe slowly nodded. "All right, that makes sense. Although I hate to see him poked with more needles."

"I know." She understood his concern. "But it's worth it if we can know for sure whether the treatment is working." She hesitated, then added, "I, uh, have to go but I'll try to check back on you later."

Gabe's exhausted, red-rimmed eyes focused on her face. "Is something wrong?"

How amazing that with everything he was going through he could still sense her own anxiety. "My mother is being admitted over at Minneapolis's Medical Center. She's fine," she added hastily, when Gabe's eyes widened in alarm, "but apparently she had a small episode of *torsades*."

"Do you want me to come with you?"

His very sincere offer touched her heart. Why did Gabe always have to be so nice? Even when he'd withheld the truth, she didn't doubt that he'd done it out of concern for her. "You stay here with JT. I'll let you know if something changes and she's not doing well."

Gabe stared at her for a moment before nodding. "If you're sure."

"I'm sure." Holly left, heading over to the large adult

teaching hospital located right next to the Children's Medical Center. As she walked, she thought it was ironic that the one man she'd thought she couldn't trust was the one who'd offered the most support, even when he was in the midst of his own personal crisis.

Maybe she'd judged him too harshly.

"Mom, how are you?" Holly asked, entering the semi-private room her mother occupied in the ED.

"Oh, I'm fine." Her mother's wan smile belied her easy tone. "Guess my heart went a little funny during my dialysis treatment."

"Yes, but it looks like your heart is doing fine now," Holly assured her, eyeing the heart monitor over the bed. Her physician's eye noted the small changes in the heart rhythm that indicated her mother may have suffered a small heart attack. Concerned, she asked, "Has your doctor been in to let you know what's going on?"

"Yes, but I told him to wait for you." Her mother clutched her hand. "Holly, I need to tell you something."

Her mother's urgent tone worried her. "What? What is it?"

"You have to forgive your father."

She frowned. Where had that come from? Had her mother suffered a lack of oxygen to her brain during the episode with her heart? Her father had been dead for eight years, although she remembered her mother saying something very similar during her father's funeral. Not that it had been easy to forgive him, when his much younger wife and daughter had sat in the front pew of the church. "Mom, don't worry about it," she soothed. "I'm fine."

"No, Holly, listen to me." Her mother tightened her grip on Holly's hand. "You haven't forgiven him, not really. Do you think I can't tell? You've been different since you've been home. There's something wrong and I think it's because you're making the same mistake with Tom."

Holly didn't know what to say. She wasn't still hung up on Tom. Gabe's lies had hurt far more.

"Don't you see? Carrying around all that resentment in your heart isn't good for you." Her mother grimaced. "Believe me, I know it's not easy, but loving a person regardless of their strengths and weaknesses will only make you a better person."

Holly bit her lip, trying to understand what her mother was saying. She already thought she was a better person than either her father or Tom—she hadn't violated her wedding vows the way they had. Yet, even as she watched, her mother's agitation made her heart rate accelerate at an alarming rate so she tried to put her feelings aside for her mother's sake.

"All right, Mom. I'll try. I'll do my best to forgive Dad and Tom."

"Don't just try, Holly. Do it. Tell yourself they were good men in their own way. Every person has good and bad traits. You have to learn to forgive them. If you don't I'm afraid you'll never find love."

Holly breathed in sharply. Why would her mother think she was looking for love? There was no way her

mother could have guessed her feelings for Gabe.
Could she?

Was her mother right? Was the resentment she
carried from the past interfering with her ability to move
into the future?

"I will, Mom," Holly said in a firm tone. "I promise
I will. Now, relax, will you? Worrying about me is putting too much stress on your heart."

Her mother relaxed, as if finally believing her.
"Thanks, Holly," she murmured. "I don't want to see
you making the same mistakes I did."

Just then the ED doctor came in and explained that
he was sending her mother over to the cath lab for a
cardiac catheterization. Holly was glad they were doing
the procedure, and within moments her mother had been
wheeled off.

Leaving Holly to wonder just what mistakes her
mother had made in the past.

Despite his worry and fear over JT, Gabe couldn't help
thinking about Holly. She'd come back briefly to
explain how her mother had suffered a small heart attack
and had undergone a procedure in the cath lab to put a
stent in a blocked coronary artery. But that had been yesterday. He hadn't seen her at all today.

He thought about walking over to Minneapolis's
Medical Center to see how her mother was doing, but
didn't like leaving JT alone.

He could call his mother to come and sit with him
for a little while. She came in every day, staying beside

JT so he could get something to eat. She'd refused to go back home to Florida, no matter how many times he'd told her to go.

Deep down he was secretly glad she'd stayed. Both his mother and Holly had given him tremendous support.

Support Holly might need in return. As much as she'd been there for him, he should do the same for her.

If she'd let him. But he wasn't sure she really wanted support from him.

"Hi, Gabe," Holly said, coming into the room as if she'd known he was thinking about her. "How's JT?"

"No change. But how is your mom?" He stood and crossed over to her. "Is she doing all right?"

"She's much better. Normally, they'd send her home after twenty-four hours, but they're going to keep her one more night, to see how she does during dialysis tomorrow."

"Great. That's great, Holly."

"We haven't heard from the CDC yet on JT's blood and spinal fluid," she told him, glancing at her watch. "I'm hoping to hear something this afternoon."

Gabe nodded. He'd been hoping the same thing. "Holly, I want you to know that no matter what happens I appreciate everything you've done for him."

"I— You're welcome. But we're not giving up yet, not by a long shot."

"I know." He was just trying to make her understand how grateful he was that she'd come back to Minneapolis just when he'd needed her most.

Not just for her expertise in treating JT but for himself on a personal level as well. He'd learned a lot sitting here, doing nothing but thinking. There was so much he wanted to say, yet the timing wasn't quite right. First he needed to know JT was on the road to recovery. Then they could talk.

Although he suspected all the talking in the world wasn't going to change the fact that Tom was JT's father. Yet there had to be a way to get through to Holly.

Because he wanted more than a professional relationship with her. He wanted it all.

The only problem was figuring out what Holly wanted.

"Dr. Davidson?" One of the PICU nurses peeked her head into the room. "I have a call for you on line one."

"Excuse me, I'll be right back." Holly hurried away.

Gabe knew the call was probably just Jeff, asking for an update. Jeff and Holly functioned as a pretty cohesive team. Yet he found himself watching Holly out at the nurses' station, talking on the phone with growing impatience.

He forced himself to look away, checking JT's vital signs displayed on the monitor. His pulse and blood pressure seemed much less labile today.

"Gabe?" Holly rushed back into the room, her eyes bright with barely restrained excitement. "JT's samples show that there's only a very minimal level of rabies virus left in his system."

He was almost afraid to ask. "So what does that mean?"

She smiled, her face lighting up the whole room. "It means it's safe to bring him out of the coma."

CHAPTER THIRTEEN

HOLLY wrote the orders to back off on JT's medications, this time at a slower rate than their first attempt. JT's pulse and blood pressure seemed to tolerate the medication changes better so she decided to take those early indicators as a good sign.

"So now we wait and hope for the best," Gabe murmured.

"Yes." She wished there was more she could do, but at the moment they needed JT's body to do the work of clearing out the medication from his bloodstream.

Some things couldn't be rushed.

She glanced at her watch, realizing it was close to the time of her mother's scheduled dialysis treatment. She glanced at Gabe. "I need to go but I'll come back later, all right?"

"Sure." Gabe smiled and for the first time in a long time she saw the hope that filled his eyes. "I'll be here."

She knew he would. Gabe hadn't left JT's bedside for any period of time longer than it took to eat a quick meal or rush home for a shower and change of clothes. He was a great father. She couldn't even believe he had harbored doubts about it before. She was beginning to think he and JT would pull through this.

Heading over to Minneapolis's Medical Center, she found the inpatient dialysis unit. The nurses were just getting her mother hooked up to the dialysis machine.

With nothing to do but wait, her mother's comments echoed over and over in her mind. She was most curious about how her mother seemed to speak from experience.

Holly finally gathered her courage to ask, "Mom, have you ever loved another man besides Dad?"

Her mother was silent for a long moment. "Yes, at least I thought I loved him. But as time went on I ended up ruining the relationship."

Holly was surprised at her mother's frank admission. "How?"

"I kept looking for reasons not to trust him." Her mother's smile was sad. "No one is perfect, Holly. Your father, Tom, they both had trouble being faithful. But they weren't bad men. Perfection doesn't exist, everyone makes mistakes if you're with them long enough. The sooner you can forgive them and move on, the better off you'll be."

"I don't know if I can," Holly confessed softly. Tom's betrayal was so wrapped up in her daughter's death she didn't know how to separate the two.

"Maybe you need to start with forgiving yourself."

Forgiving herself? She stared at her mother, perplexed. "What do you mean?"

"Holly, I've been there. I know how easy it is to blame

yourself for not seeing through the charming veneer to the man beneath." Her mother grimaced. "You have to forgive yourself for marrying the wrong man, and that's not easy to do. You must have thought you were in love with Tom to agree to marry him in the first place."

"Yes." Her mother's words struck a chord. She had wallowed in guilt for making a bad choice, especially after nearly kissing Gabe before the wedding. Maybe if she had been more honest with herself, acknowledging her feelings earlier, she could have avoided her marriage and subsequent divorce.

But that also meant not having had Kayla, even for those brief moments. And no matter how much she considered her marriage to Tom a mistake, she couldn't consider her daughter to be one, too.

"I think I knew Tom was wrong for me even before I married him," she whispered, speaking the truth out loud for the first time in years. "And you're right, I blamed myself for not being strong enough to break things off then."

"Yes. I had a similar experience." Her mother reached over with her good hand, the one not connected to the dialysis machine, to give Holly's a squeeze. "But I couldn't regret my marriage either, because of you. You gave me something to live for. Something to be strong for. I just wished I could have come to terms with my anger and resentment toward your father much quicker."

So she could move on with someone else? "Who was he?" Holly asked, honestly curious. While she'd still been in high school, she hadn't been aware of her mother dating anyone. Not that she'd been very aware of her mother's problems back then, she thought with a pang of guilt.

"His name was Scott Anderson and I met him through a divorce support group a couple of years ago."

A support group. After all these years? She hadn't even realized her mother had been to one. "So what happened? Are you still in touch with him?"

"Not really, not since I've been sick enough to need dialysis." Her mother waved a hand impatiently. "Why are we talking about me? This is supposed to be about you."

Holly could see what had happened, the way her mother had broken off communication with Scott after she'd discovered her renal failure had meant she'd need to go on dialysis. Knowing her mother, she hadn't wanted Scott to consider her a burden.

"Tell you what, Mom. I'll work on forgiving myself and Tom if you get in touch with Scott. Has it occurred to you he might be worried about you, even as a friend?"

Her mother was quiet for a long moment. "Yes, it's occurred to me."

"So?" Holly persisted. "That means you could at least call him, right?"

"Right," her mother sighed. "It's a deal."

"Good." Holly sat back in her seat, satisfied. Maybe it was too late for Scott and her mother, but even if there was nothing left of the relationship other than friendship, that wouldn't be so bad either.

Friends and family were important.

She thought of Gabe, standing watch over JT. The

boy was still clinging to life, like some sort of tiny miracle. Discovering the truth about who JT's biological father was didn't change anything. JT was still more Gabe's son than anyone else's.

Had she done the same thing her mother had?

Had she deliberately looked for a reason not to trust Gabe?

Gabe had always known patience wasn't his area of greatest strength. Forty-eight hours had passed since Holly and Jeff had started decreasing JT's medication. Last night they'd turned everything off completely.

But JT still hadn't woken up.

He stared at his clasped hands dangling between his knees, battling a feeling of impending doom. What if all this treatment had been for nothing? What if JT never woke up from his coma?

Days ago he'd thought he'd be satisfied to know JT was alive, but as he stared down at his son's youthful face he had to admit he'd lied to himself. Because he wanted more than for JT to simply exist with a stable heart rate and a blood pressure.

He wanted JT to recover enough to be aware of his surroundings. To talk. To walk. To climb trees, swing-sets or whatever else he wanted to climb.

To someday go back to school.

He wanted it all. Not necessarily right away, he could be patient for a little while. But he definitely wanted it all. JT's recovery.

And more. He wanted the impossible.

Holly entered JT's room and he dragged his gaze up to meet hers. "Nothing yet?" she asked.

Slowly he shook his head.

She let out a sigh. "Hang in there, Gabe. You know there is so much we don't know about the brain. The good news is that he's been off all his medication since last night. It may just take a while for him to wake up, that's all."

He couldn't make himself smile. "I know. Logically, I know this may take a while. And he might not even recognize anyone when he does wake up. But it's hard. We've been waiting for so long."

"I know." She moved over to JT's bedside to perform a brief neuro exam. "His pupils are equal and reactive to light," she murmured.

He nodded, knowing fully well, as she did, that JT's pupil response didn't mean anything. All it meant was that his brain hadn't totally shut down. "How long before you do an EEG?"

Holly's glance was surprised. "Has Jeff mentioned doing one?" she asked, avoiding a direct answer.

Gabe lifted a shoulder. "No, but I figured it's only a matter of time. Once the meds have cleared his system, there should be no reason for him not to wake up. Unless his brain is having deep, underlying seizure activity that we're not aware of." Some seizures were so deep, so primitive, they didn't show obvious signs and symptoms.

"We'll give him a few days yet," Holly assured him. "I don't think he's having seizures."

"But the only way to know for sure is to do an EEG," Gabe persisted.

"Yes." She reached over to rest her hand lightly on his shoulder. "Give him some time, Gabe. The virus has been a huge stress on his system. Give him time to wake up on his own."

He took a deep breath and let it out slowly. "Okay. You're right, it's still early." It was ridiculous to be so disappointed that JT didn't immediately open his eyes and look at him, fully aware of his surroundings.

"It is early," Holly agreed. "And we already know that most of the virus is no longer in his system."

Gabe didn't answer. Because he'd read the case studies for himself. Most of the patients had died from other complications, not from the virus itself. In JT's case there could be complications from the coma.

He prayed JT wouldn't be another rabies casualty.

On Monday morning, three full days after they'd stopped all JT's medications, Gabe watched as numerous tiny electrodes were glued to JT's scalp. His eyes burned from exhaustion, but still he couldn't look away.

Three days and JT hadn't woken up.

Gabe was certain there was something serious wrong. Jeff and Holly kept saying to give him time— they'd even taken the breathing tube out—but all he could think was that JT must be having deep seizure activity in order to explain why he hadn't come around from the coma.

"There, last one," the tech said cheerfully. She didn't seem to mind that JT didn't respond, she'd gone on to explain what she was doing anyway.

Gabe stared at the young woman with dull eyes. Irrationally, he wanted to yell at her to stop being so perky. Couldn't she tell JT was going to die? Couldn't she see that everything they'd done had been for nothing?

He wished Holly was there. He needed her to stand beside him if he was going to lose JT.

"Hmm," the tech said, as she started up the machine, watching as JT's brain waves were being monitored by the tiny needles. "Interesting."

He wasn't an expert on reading EEGs but he leaned forward to look at the small zig-zag scribbles the numerous needles were making on the wide graph paper anyway. The device looked primitive, something akin to a seismograph measuring earthquake activities. After all these years of modern advances in healthcare, it seemed as if there should be a better, more technical way to measure brain waves.

"What?" he asked. The scribbles on the paper made no sense to him. "Is he having seizures?"

"I'm just the tech," she said primly. "I'm not qualified to make medical judgments."

He clenched his fingers into fists, controlling his temper with an effort. If she wasn't qualified to make medical judgments, why had she even said anything? And what was so interesting? "Where's Jeff Konen?"

The girl had the grace to look guilty. "I don't know, but I can page him if you like."

"Page him," Gabe said between clenched teeth. He wanted to know if JT was having seizures and he wanted to know now.

Seeing the grim expression on his face, the tech hurried away. The machine continued to roll, like a giant lie detector, the needles scribbling on the paper like a kid scraping his nails down a chalkboard.

Gabe was still staring at the paper when the tech returned with Jeff in tow.

"Gabe," Jeff said by way of greeting. Jeff moved over to glance down at the long page of brain waves already documented by the EEG machine. "So far this looks good."

"Good?" Gabe grasped on the positive note. "You mean he's not having seizures?"

"No seizures—at least, not so far," Jeff confirmed. "Typically we run the test for a good hour, though. Now, calm down, all right? You're scaring the tech."

Gabe hunched his shoulders. "She started it," he mumbled, knowing he sounded ridiculous. After weeks of sitting at JT's side, he felt as if he was close to losing it.

JT's hand moved in a jerky motion. Gabe blinked, wondering if his exhausted brain had imagined it. Then JT's hand moved again, this time as if he was trying to raise his hand off the bed.

"JT?" he called, crossing over to JT's bed. He took the boy's small hand in his. JT's hand moved again, another jerky movement, not a hand grasp by any stretch of the imagination. "Jeff, do you think this might be residual seizure activity?"

"No, you have to remember rabies affects the nervous system. His muscles may not move normally for quite a while yet."

Gabe nodded, clinging to JT's hand. The jerky movements stopped. He willed them back.

The tech finished the EEG and quickly disconnected all the electrodes from JT's scalp. The poor kid looked like some sort of mini-rock star with globs of white goop still matted in his hair, which stuck out from his head at odd angles.

"We'll get that gunk out of your hair, JT, don't worry," the nurse said when she came in a few minutes later. "I found some stuff that works really well."

JT turned his head toward the sound of her voice.

Gabe swallowed hard. There was a loud buzzing in his ears and his heart thundered in his chest. He clung to JT's hand as if it were a lifeline.

"JT?" He had to clear the hoarseness from his throat. "Hey, buddy, it's me, Uncle Gabe. I'm here with you, JT. You've been sick but you're getting better." From the corner of his eye he noticed both Holly and Jeff walk into the room as if curious to see if JT would finally wake up. The PICU nurse stood on one side of the bed, while he stayed on the opposite side. "JT, can you open your eyes for me? Can you see me?"

JT's hand jerked in his, and Gabe held his breath, almost afraid to hope. JT's other hand jerked, as did his feet, but the motions weren't synchronized, as if JT was having trouble getting his muscles to obey his commands.

"Take your time, buddy," Gabe said, even though he was sure more waiting would kill him. "We're not going anywhere. We have all the time in the world."

JT opened his eyes, blinked and then closed them again.

"Dim the lights," Gabe said harshly.

Holly crossed over to dim the fluorescent overhead lights.

"There, JT, the lights aren't so bright now," Gabe said in a reassuring tone. "Can you open your eyes for me? Can you look at me, JT?"

JT turned his head toward the sound of Gabe's voice. Gabe felt Holly and Jeff come up to stand on either side of him. He barely glanced at them, having eyes only for JT.

"He's never seen Jeff, so we need to make sure he can differentiate between you," Holly said in a low tone.

Gabe understood what she was saying. They needed to know if JT was really in there, able to recognize his surroundings. Able to recognize *him*.

JT opened his eyes again, and Gabe's hopes plummeted when it seemed at first as if JT was gazing at nothing, not even the pretty PICU nurse standing on the other side of the bed. But then, slowly, the boy moved his gaze toward Gabe.

"Welcome back, JT," Holly said, her voice thick with suppressed tears. "You've been sick, but you're much better now. We've all been worried about you."

JT's gaze moved from Holly to Gabe and then to Jeff, with no moment of recognition from what Gabe could tell. But then JT's gaze came back to focus on Gabe. His mouth moved and he tried to speak.

"Da-ddy?"

Gabe stared at JT, wondering if he'd really heard the

somewhat garbled word right. Holly's tremulous smile convinced him he had.

JT had not only recognized him, he'd called him Daddy.

CHAPTER FOURTEEN

HOLLY'S eyes filled with tears even as her heart soared with excitement. JT had finally awoken from his coma.

JT had called Gabe Daddy.

The treatment to combat his illness had worked.

"JT, I love you, son. I love you so much." Gabe was crying but seemed not to notice as he gathered the boy in his arms. JT tried to talk again as he cuddled against Gabe's chest as if seeking comfort, but much of his speech was garbled, except for one word that was quickly becoming very clear.

Daddy.

"He's awake. Can you believe it? JT's awake," Holly heard one of the PICU nurses say excitedly.

A ripple of celebration went through the whole unit. Several of the staff, nurses and physicians and techs, came to stand at JT's door, some of them smiling, others wiping away tears.

Gabe just continued to hold his son, smoothing a hand down the boy's back. Holly blinked away her tears of happiness. JT had recognized Gabe, though the rest of his recovery would come more slowly. Youth was on his side.

And there was no rush. JT could take all the time he needed to return to his usual self. The boy had his whole life ahead of him.

"We did it," Jeff murmured, a sense of awe in his tone. "I can't believe we got him through this."

"Love is what got him through this," Holly corrected, unable to tear her gaze from the way Gabe cradled JT close.

"Yeah. You're probably right." Jeff was grinning like an idiot. "But we helped a little."

"We helped a little," Holly agreed. She turned away, feeling a little too much like an outsider. Gabe had his son back. There was no doubt in her mind that JT would continue to recover.

Gabe didn't need Holly's help anymore.

She was glad, fiercely glad that JT had pulled through the horrible virus that had wreaked havoc on his small body. She was happy he was stable enough not to need the acute level of care the peds ICU provided.

Still, she left JT's room, feeling as if her professional job was done.

But also feeling that, just like her mother, she'd somehow ruined her chance for personal happiness with JT and Gabe.

Holly continued to keep an eye on JT's progress. The whole hospital did. JT's survival was the main topic of conversation. By the end of the following week JT was talking better but his language skills came back slowly.

"Holly, I've been waiting for you," Gabe said when she showed up at the end of her day. She was busier than usual, thanks in part to being touted by the CDC as one of the experts in treating rabies. Her colleague was a greater expert than she could ever be, but she didn't mind answering questions from other doctors across the country.

"Good news." Gabe's grin was infectious. "JT's being transferred to Rehab in the morning."

"That's wonderful." She smiled at JT. "First rehab, then the next step is going home. I bet you're going to make your rehab nurses chase you down the hall, aren't you?"

"Don't give him any ideas," Gabe warned half under his breath. "He's already faster in his wheelchair than I can keep up with."

"Sorry," she said with a smile. JT's muscles still didn't always work the way he wanted them to, but the good thing about being a kid was that learning to walk again was easier than it would be as an adult. Soon he'd graduate from the wheelchair to leg braces.

Hopefully JT would be back on his feet, climbing the nearest tree.

"You're not going to sign off on JT's care, are you?" Gabe asked.

She nodded. "Yes, actually, I am. Rehab isn't the same as inpatient treatment. Jeff will continue to follow JT's progress in the clinic, but from here on you don't need me." She hoped her tone didn't sound as dejected as she felt.

"I guess that's a good sign in and of itself," Gabe mused.

Oh, boy, she wished she felt the same way. But she'd always known Gabe didn't need her anymore. Not as far as JT's treatment was concerned.

Maybe not as far as anything else was concerned either.

"Actually, that helps because I was hoping you'd have dinner with me," Gabe said, glancing at his watch. "Tonight. If you're not doing anything."

Dinner? Tonight? Deep in the darkest corner of her heart a flicker of hope flared. Still, she hesitated. "Are you sure? I thought… Aren't you spending the nights here, at the hospital?"

"I've been leaving lately," Gabe said slowly. "Needed to make sure the place was ready for when JT comes home."

She knew Gabe hadn't been back to work yet, but suspected he'd need to return soon. Her tiny flare of hope dimmed. Maybe he was going to ask for help with JT. After all, she'd offered.

And at this point she'd probably take whatever she could get.

"Have to pay my bills. Wouldn't be good if the power company shut off my electricity, now, would it?" Gabe joked.

"No, it wouldn't be good to be without electricity." There was no reason to avoid having dinner with him. So much had happened in the weeks since JT was so sick that they had to start somewhere. "I'd love to have dinner with you," she said abruptly.

Gabe's eyes widened in surprise but he grinned. "Great. I, uh, thought we could try Giovani's. According to my mother's expert opinion, it's the only decent Italian place around."

"Perfect." She wasn't about to argue, especially not with an Italian cook like Gabe's mother. "How is she, by the way?"

"She went home, but she promised to return for a while once JT is released from the hospital."

She couldn't help raising a brow. If he had his mother's help, maybe he didn't need hers. "Great."

"And Marybeth is recovering from her surgery. She's been in to visit JT, too." It was as if Gabe had read her mind, putting all her misplaced fears to rest. "Are you ready to leave now? Or do you have more patients to see?"

Suddenly she didn't feel very ready, but she nodded. "No more patients to see. JT's my last one." And it was officially her last visit as JT's infectious disease doctor. She took JT's hand in hers. "Glad to see you're doing so much better, JT."

"Better," he repeated.

She smiled. "Be good to the nurses in Rehab, you hear? The sooner you do what they tell you, the sooner you'll go home, okay?"

This time he simply nodded.

"Bye, JT." She squeezed his hand and let go.

"Bye, Dr. Holly. See you soon." JT's stilted speech, stringing six whole words together in two distinct sentences, sounded like music from the finest symphony. She had absolutely no doubt he'd get the rest of his vocabulary back soon.

"Are you ready to go, then?" Gabe asked, his hand resting on her lower back.

Her stomach fluttered but she forced herself to nod. "Yes. I'm ready."

Gabe finally had Holly all to himself, yet he was already having doubts about his plan. Maybe because he was having trouble figuring her out. Her attitude toward JT seemed the same as it had been before she'd known who his biological father was.

Did that mean she didn't care about Tom's affair with his sister? Or did it mean she was treating JT only as a patient and not as a child she might someday call her own?

He wished he knew what she saw when she looked at his son, but he didn't.

And he wasn't sure how to ask.

He hiked his jeans a little self-consciously as they made their way down the elevator to the lobby level. He'd lost a bit of weight through the time of JT's illness and figured eating a good Italian meal was one way to help pack the carbohydrates back on.

Besides, he had been remiss in not taking Holly out for a proper date sooner.

There were a lot of things he should have done. Not least of which was to tell her how he really felt.

"I'm glad to see you're getting out of the hospital, at least for a little while," Holly commented as he walked her toward his car. "How much longer will you be off work?"

"Just a couple of weeks. JT should be home soon and

then we'll get things back into a normal routine." A normal routine that he knew very well would consist of a lot of physical therapy, speech therapy and a variety of other doctors' appointments.

A fresh wave of doubt hit him. What was he thinking? Maybe he was committed to being JT's father, but what right did he have to ask Holly to share in any of this? They'd only made love that one night, maybe he was crazy to be thinking about a future.

Even if visions of the future were the only thing that had kept him sane over these past few weeks.

"It's amazing that he pulled through, isn't it?" Holly said, settling in the passenger seat of his car.

"Yes." Gabe had to hide his momentary flash of annoyance. For once he didn't want to talk about JT. Call him selfish, but for a brief hour he wanted to talk about something else.

About Holly. About the wonderful feelings that had bloomed between them when they'd made love.

And more than anything he wanted to know if there was anything left between them to build on?

He swallowed hard and concentrated on driving. His mother's opinion proved to be correct—Giovani's was a great place. Once they were seated in a romantic corner, he felt a little of his determination return. He ordered a bottle of wine and took a sip to hide his nervousness.

"Holly," he began, after the waiter had taken their order. "I know it's been a long time since the night I spent at your place, but I still think about those hours with you a lot."

A ghost of a smile played along her mouth. "Me, too. At this point it seems like more a dream."

More of a dream than reality? Not a positive note to move forward with. He frowned, and wondered if he ought to try another approach. "One thing I realized, sitting with JT, is that life is meant to be shared. You were the main reason I was able to keep going, even when JT was at his worst."

"Me?" She toyed with her wineglass. Was she nervous about this, too? "I don't understand."

Gabe scrubbed a hand over his face and decided this beating around the bush was useless. Better to get straight to the point. "I love you. I knew I'd fallen in love with you that first night we spent together. But then JT was so sick I didn't have a chance to tell you how I felt." Since he was being honest, he amended that latter part by adding, "I didn't take the time to tell you how I really felt."

Her mouth opened, and closed, no words coming out. Holly wasn't often speechless.

"But this isn't just about us," he continued slowly. "JT is officially my son. I received approval from the adoption agency this morning. So the real question here is about you, Holly. I guess I need to know if you're ever going to be able to accept JT for who he is."

There was a long moment of silence when his confidence wavered. He understood he was asking for a lot.

"Yes," Holly finally said in a soft but decisive tone. "Gabe, I love JT as much as you do. I could never hold his genes against him, any more than I could have held it against Kayla."

Hope flared, burning brightly in the center of his chest. "But Kayla was your daughter, too."

"I know. But what made her my daughter? Simply giving birth? I don't think so. What makes JT your son?"

Was this a test? He'd hated quizzes in medical school. "Love?" he guessed.

"Love." A tremulous smile curved her lips. "Love is what makes the relationship between a parent and their child special. Just like love is what holds a relationship between a husband and a wife together. With love anything is possible."

The truth shone from her eyes and he considered himself the luckiest man on earth to have found a woman like Holly. He reached for her hand, suddenly wishing he hadn't chosen a public place like Giovani's to talk to her. "Are you sure? Because if not I'll give you time. As much time as you need."

"I'm sure." Holly's smile widened. "I've learned a lot over these past few weeks, too. The biggest thing I've learned is that I probably started falling in love with you a long time ago. The night I almost kissed you."

That was good, wasn't it? He wasn't sure. But then he decided that as he'd come this far, he'd better go all the way. "Does that mean you'll marry me?"

"Yes, Gabe." Her fingers curled tightly around his. "I love you. I'd be honored to marry you."

He didn't have a ring, but somehow he didn't think Holly cared. He rose to his feet and came around to her side of the table, drawing her up, too. Pulling her close, he kissed her. Then, when he could hear the whispers moving through the restaurant behind him, he broke off the kiss and turned to the group and boldly declared, "Holly Davidson has just agreed to be my wife."

It wasn't until a ripple of applause and wolf-whistles surrounded them that he realized what he'd done. Holly hated being in the limelight. She didn't like being the center of gossip.

"Damn. What was I thinking? I'm sorry," he tried to backpedal to undo the damage he might have unwittingly done, turning back to wave at the people in the restaurant, trying to shut them up.

Holly grabbed his arm, laughing. "For heaven's sake, don't be sorry. I'm proud I'm going to be your wife."

Relief flooded him. He hadn't ruined things between them after all. "Good, that's good." Why couldn't he think of something more intelligent to say?

"Gabe." She tugged on his hand until he stepped closer. She lifted her mouth to his, teasing his lips with hers. "After dinner, will you take me home?"

"Yes." That's exactly what he wanted, too. A whole night, all to themselves. "I'll take you home, tonight and forever."

Home had never sounded so good.

EPILOGUE

JT FROWNED when his daddy leaned down to let him look at his new baby brother. He wasn't going to say anything, but he thought there might be something wrong because the baby's face looked all red and wrinkly.

"Isn't he amazing?" his daddy asked.

"Yeah. Amazing." JT didn't quite understand what was so amazing, although it was weird that one minute his new mom's tummy was huge and now it wasn't big anymore but there was a baby.

What he really wanted to know was how that baby got in there in the first place. And were there any more babies in there, ready to come out? If so, maybe he should ask for a sister.

"We thought we'd name him Jeffery, after the doctor who helped make you all better," his new mom said.

"Holly, you were a part of the medical team, too," his dad argued, but when his mom gave him an exasperated look he lifted his hands in the air. "But if that's what you want, Jeffery it is."

Jeffery didn't sound like a bad name. "Hi, Jeffery," he said to the baby.

His dad rested a hand on his shoulder. "How do you think you'll like being a big brother, JT?" his dad asked.

He glanced up at his dad and then over at his mom. They were both looking at him as if they were afraid of what he might say.

The baby didn't look like he'd be able to run and play any time soon. Which was probably okay as he couldn't run very well with the leg braces on. But he knew what they were really asking him.

"Why? Are there more kids inside Mom waiting to be born?"

His parents looked at each other and burst into laughter. They laughed until they were crying but he wasn't sure what was so funny.

"Uh, yeah. Maybe. There might be more kids in there waiting to be born," his dad finally said.

It figured. He sighed. He loved his dad and his mom. He figured he'd learn to love Jeffery and any other kids that came out of his mom's tummy.

He knew he was lucky to have a family.

"Then I guess I like being a big brother just fine."

From governess to mother and wife!

Two brand-new heartwarming historical
romances featuring:

More Than a Governess by Sarah Mallory
The Angel and the Outlaw by Kathryn Albright

**The special gift of a mother's love.
Perfect reading for Mother's Day!**

Available 6th March 2009

www.millsandboon.co.uk

M&B

4 Books
and a surprise gift!

We would like to take this opportunity to thank you for reading this Mills & Boon® book by offering you the chance to take FOUR more specially selected titles from the Medical™ series absolutely FREE! We're also making this offer to introduce you to the benefits of the Mills & Boon® Book Club™ —

- ★ **FREE home delivery**
- ★ **FREE gifts and competitions**
- ★ **FREE monthly Newsletter**
- ★ **Exclusive Mills & Boon Book Club offers**
- ★ **Books available before they're in the shops**

Accepting these FREE books and gift places you under no obligation to buy, you may cancel at any time, even after receiving your free shipment. Simply complete your details below and return the entire page to the address below. You don't even need a stamp!

YES! Please send me 4 free Medical books and a surprise gift. I understand that unless you hear from me, I will receive 6 superb new titles every month for just £2.99 each, postage and packing free. I am under no obligation to purchase any books and may cancel my subscription at any time. The free books and gift will be mine to keep in any case.

M9ZEF

Ms/Mrs/Miss/Mr .... Initials ....
BLOCK CAPITALS PLEASE

Surname ....

Address ....

....

.... Postcode ....

Send this whole page to:
UK: FREEPOST CN81, Croydon, CR9 3WZ

FREE BOOKS OFFER

To get you started, we'll send you
2 FREE books and a FREE gift

There's no catch, everything is **FREE**

Accepting your 2 **FREE** books and **FREE** mystery gift
places you under no obligation to buy anything.

Be part of the Mills & Boon® Book Club™ and receive your favourite
Series books up to 2 months before they are in the shops and delivered
straight to your door. Plus, enjoy a wide range of **EXCLUSIVE** benefits!

- Best new women's fiction – delivered right to
  your door with FREE P&P

- Avoid disappointment – get your books up to
  2 months before they are in the shops

- No contract – no obligation to buy

2 **FREE** books
and a
FREE gift

We hope that after receiving your free books you'll
want to remain a member. But the choice is yours.
So why not give us a go? You'll be glad you did!

Visit **millsandboon.co.uk** to stay up to date
with offers and to sign-up for our newsletter

M9CI

Mrs/Miss/Ms/Mr	Initials	

BLOCK CAPITALS PLEASE

Surname

Address

Postcode

Email

MILLS & BOON®
Book Club

FREE BOOK OFFER
FREEPOST CN81
CROYDON
CR9 3WZ

NO STAMP
NECESSARY
IF POSTED IN
THE U.K. OR N.I.